DETECTIVE STORIES

I Fear the Greeks

by Aaron Marc Stein

I FEAR THE GREEKS
BLOOD ON THE STARS
HOME AND MURDER
NEVER NEED AN ENEMY
SITTING UP DEAD
MOONMILK AND MURDER
DEATH MEETS 400 RABBITS
THE DEAD THING IN THE POOL
MASK FOR MURDER
PISTOLS FOR TWO
SHOOT ME DACENT
FRIGHTENED AMAZON
THREE—WITH BLOOD
DAYS OF MISFORTUNE
THE SECOND BURIAL
THE CRADLE AND THE GRAVE
DEATH TAKES A PAYING GUEST
WE SAW HIM DIE
. . . AND HIGH WATER
CASE OF THE ABSENT-MINDED PROFESSOR
ONLY THE GUILTY
UP TO NO GOOD
THE SUN IS A WITNESS
HER BODY SPEAKS
SPIRALS

A CRIME CLUB SELECTION

Without ever looking for it, a man can find trouble anywhere, and there are some who will tell you that just going to Cairo or to Athens is looking for trouble. For Matt Erridge that's about the way the trouble started. He just went. Regardless of place, though, anyone will tell you that a good way to find trouble is to get involved with a woman, and that is also what Matt Erridge did. This time, however, the woman was his mother, and shouldn't that have been safe enough? Mom, never sweeter and never more gentle, tells him that she's arranged everything for him. What's he to think when the arrangements include slugging and drugging?

And then it's murder, and all at the hands of total strangers.

SCENE: *Cairo and Athens*

 Favorite Sleuth

AARON MARC STEIN

I Fear the Greeks

PUBLISHED FOR THE CRIME CLUB BY

DOUBLEDAY & COMPANY, INC.   GARDEN CITY, NEW YORK

1966

All of the characters in this book are fictitious,
and any resemblance to actual persons, living or
dead, is purely coincidental.

TO
MIRIAM-ANN HAGEN
AND
ΠΑΛΛΑΣ ΑΘΗΝΗ

I Fear the Greeks

I

I had been working. It was in the vicinity of the Persian Gulf. It was the back gate to nowhere. It was the whole of eternity converted into one non-stop, hot afternoon. It was one of those sons of the desert who fits a fleet of air-conditioned Cadillacs into his tenth-century world and keeps his people equally flexible. He rides the Cadillacs without losing any of his ancient and honorable essence. So now if Matt Erridge will build him a Cadillac of oil refineries, surely his people can sweat around in that without losing any of theirs. He wants it modern, but not too compact. Have to give the overseers that extra bit of room for swinging the whips.

It was the fifth time in as many months that the whole deal had bogged down in bombast, bunk, and bakshish. I'd sweated out the other four times, but now it was spring. Other places trees were coming into leaf, birds were sitting on eggs, tulips were spearing up out of the earth, lambs were frolicking, and men were feeling again that good old rising of the sap. Where I was, it was still sun, sweat, stink, and Cadillacs. No place but inside himself could Erridge detect anything of the annual transformation.

Even before Mom came into it, I had the itch to up and go some place where I could do a little celebrating of those age-old rites of spring. Are you asking how come a grown man, afflicted with that itch, goes running to his mother?

I'm not knocking motherhood, you understand. Say what you

like about Erridge, but never say of him that he doesn't dig motherhood, but great. It's just that a boy, once he's grown, gets departmentalized, and the rites of spring department is one of those the boy's best friend doesn't come into. It's the Great Earth Mom who has the monopoly on that one.

I'm not knocking my own mom either. Quite simply, she's the most, but how come she lands me in all this grief? It's spring. I'm on the other side of nowhere, dodging sun, intrigue, and flies. Mom's back home watching her garden come up and going along as she always did. What made the difference was she read a book.

Now it wasn't as though she isn't always reading books. She's a literate woman, and she works at it all the time. You want an opinion on anything from *Little Women* to *Fanny Hill*, just ask Mom. She's read them all. This particular book, however, was special. It made her ask herself what if she wasn't home to see her tulips come up. Year after year she'd seen the garden, and she'd never even once seen Athens and Aegina, Marathon and Mycenae, Delos and Delphi, Corinth and Crete. So all of a sudden nothing else will do. Mom has to take off for Greece.

She flies to Athens. She hires herself a car. She hits the road. She is an indomitable woman, but if there is anything that will ever dim the Glory that is Greece, it's Athenian traffic. You know about traffic?

You don't know about Athens. There it has that little extra something. Athens has buses—tourist buses, urban and interurban buses, buses to take people down to the Piraeus to board the cruise boats. It also has one-way streets. All bus doors are on the right-hand side. All access to luggage compartments is on the right-hand side. They never pull up to park but on the left-hand side of the street. Get the picture?

You're in the traffic, trying to go by. You're also in a hired heap, which means a motor vehicle of unpredictable habits. Looks like you have enough problems, doesn't it? So in Athens you also have to contend with tourists on the hoof. In thundering herds they come around their bus, cameras swinging, eyes rolling, stiletto heels wobbling.

They fight their way to the bus door. There they always get stuck. It can be a camera strap looping over the door handle. It can be a too narrow skirt and a too high step. It can be the bus driver running through a countdown on his controls and hitting the lever that shuts the door in the face of an embarking tourist. It can be the dame who finds two people between herself and her husband and fights it like divorce.

All this is happening not on the sidewalk, but out on the right-hand side of that bus that has parked itself to the left. It's happening under the nose of your hired heap. Strong men turn as white as yoghurt.

Maybe it wasn't Mom at all who put me into this spot of trouble. Maybe it was Fate, because Fate picked the moment when old, hard-bitten Matt came all over filial and phoned Mom's Athens hotel just to chat. Fresh from a palaver with his son of the desert, old, hard-bitten Matt had been bitten too hard. He was itching with boredom, and then Mom, right from the first word, didn't sound like herself. Her voice was way up there where everything goes shrill and shaky.

I asked her how she was, and she said she was fine, and how was I? I told her never better except for worrying about her.

"Worrying about me?" she shrilled. "It's a lovely hotel. What's to worry about?"

"Just listen to yourself, baby," I told her. "Harness your shakes, and they'll whip cream."

"I'm lying down," she quavered.

"With a cold towel on your head?"

"Not at the phone. I could get electrocuted."

"You're changing the subject," I said.

"What was the subject?" she asked.

"What's wrong with you? That's the subject."

"I'm a bit nervous. I'll get over it."

"Over what?"

"There was this man. I knocked him down."

"Fisticuffs?"

"Don't be silly, Matthew. Actually it was his wife who knocked him down, but if it hadn't been for me, she wouldn't have. You understand?"

"Since it's you," I said, "no. You and this man are having a thing. His wife doesn't care for it. She swings on him. He goes down. Considering your looks, baby, no man can be blamed; but I know you. You don't go for it."

"Matthew," she said. "You are silly."

"Okay, baby," I said. "You've been married, and I haven't. Try to make it simpler for me. I'm your inexperienced boy, Mom."

"She didn't mean to."

"Didn't mean to what?"

"Didn't mean to knock him down. She was upset, and it's not as though anybody was injured or anything like that. It's just that I've lost my nerve. I may never be able to drive again. Certainly not in this country."

"Oh," I said. "Try it simply and consecutively, like filling out the insurance report."

She was driving down one of those one-way streets. She swears they came from nowhere. First it was a pyramid of luggage sitting out in the middle of the street. Next it was a taxi with the maniacal illusion that it was as slim-hipped as a bicycle. The taxi was trying to twist past her where there was no twisting room. Finally it was the women. They were the ones who came from nowhere and in a swarm.

"It seemed as though they were all over me, Matthew," Mom said, "with their knit dresses and their little white gloves and their hairnets."

Mom did concede that even if they hadn't been wearing the little white gloves and the hairnets, the situation would still have been unmanageable; but she insisted that the gloves and the hairnets made the difference between the merely impossible and the completely nightmarish.

So inevitably one of these dames stampeded straight across Mom's bow, and it was either nudging the babe or crunching into the taxi. Contact with the cab could produce nothing but one of those chain-reaction smashups that would have reached all the way from Syntagma Square to the most tangled depths of the Plaka. Mom nudged the babe.

Happily nothing in the whole snarl had much velocity going for it except those stampeding heifers in the gloves and the hair-nets. So this dame bounced harmlessly off the nose of Mom's heap. Lacking bouncing room, she bounced straight into her husband, and he went down.

"Actually, Matt," Mom told me, "I did make the right choice. Nobody was hurt. That woman was pretty nasty, but it was to be expected from a woman like that. She actually had her hair on pink rollers under that hairnet; but everyone else was charming, the taxi man, the bus driver, the woman's husband who wasn't hurt the least little bit, and even the police." She paused to drag in what sounded like a long, shuddering breath. "Oh, dear," she moaned, "that policeman."

"So what's with 'that policeman'?"

Now she was talking fast. "He was really very kind, and he couldn't have been more considerate," she said. "He saw I was much too shaken even to drive around to the hotel. He took the wheel and drove me home."

"Very nice," I said, "but I repeat. What's with 'that police-man'?"

"Matt," she burbled and I could tell that she was thinking as fast as she was talking. "Matt, his driving. It's a miracle he didn't kill us both."

"You're changing the subject again," I insisted. "His driving didn't get you all that worked up. You've driven with me, after all. The Greek fuzz gave you a wild ride back to the hotel. Then what?"

"Nothing, Matthew. He's just trying to be kind."

I was on to it like a bird dog. "He *is* just trying to be kind," I quoted. "Not 'was,' '*is*.'"

Her answer was quick. I dug right off it was too quick. I wasn't to go pouncing on her English that way. So she said "is" when she meant "was." She was in Greece, and she had been struggling with Greek, a language studded with booby traps.

" 'Yes' sounds like 'nay,' " she explained, "and 'no' sounds like 'okay.' For B they write MP because their B isn't B any more. It's V, except that sometimes MP isn't B because it's really MP. Small wonder my English has come just the tiniest bit unhinged."

I wasn't buying it. "Just a little tension," I said, "hitting you in the tenses. You're talking to your boy, Matthew, baby. Matthew learned his English at your knee. He knows it doesn't unhinge that easy."

She was right in there with the protest. " 'Fuzz,' " she said, "and 'dig.' Don't say you learned that kind of English at my knee."

"Where did you pick up this bad habit of changing the subject all the time? Give, baby. What's with the Greek fuzz?"

"He patted me. I think he meant it to be reassuring."

"But it wasn't. Where did he pat you?"

"I'm not going to answer silly questions."

"Oh, there."

"Yes, there."

"Am I supposed to be shocked? You are very nice, you know. You will go on looking younger and more beautiful all the time. You're in a part of the world where dames wither at half your age. Come to think of it, if you weren't my mother . . ."

"Stop thinking of it. It's indecent."

"I can remember Pop used to."

"That's just it. Nobody has since. It's unsettling."

"He meant it as a compliment." For calming her down it was the wrong thing to say.

"Oh, Matthew," she wailed. "That's just the trouble. He's on duty tonight, but tomorrow he has the night off. He's coming around. He wants to show me the Athens the tourists never see."

"But you said no?"

"Of course, I said no."

"And you're not sure you made it stick?"

"Matthew, I know I didn't make it stick. We were right out in the lobby with every American in Greece looking at us, and he said he knew how upset and unnerved I was. He said that after a good night's rest and a nice, quiet day—he recommended an afternoon at the pool followed by a couple of hours with the hotel masseuse and hairdresser—he knew I would feel completely myself again. Tomorrow evening, he said. He'd be out of uniform, he said; and there was something about the way he said 'out of uniform' that gave me the feeling he meant not into anything else. Then right there in the hotel lobby with all those harpies smoothing their little white gloves and staring at us from under their hairnets, he did it again."

"Patted you?"

"Yes."

"In the same old place?"

"Where else?"

"Could be he's been overdoing it."

"He means it to be reassuring."

"Is it reassuring?"

"You know it isn't."

"So leave us not snow ourselves, baby."

"Matthew, I'd rather be dead than the silly sort of aging female who imagines every man is making advances to her."

"Don't let that bug you till you start looking like an aging female."

"What can I do about him?"

"Tell the desk that, if anyone asks for you, you're out."

"Greek desk clerks don't lie to policemen, Matthew."

"Be out."

"All night?"

"He'll be that persistent?"

"He'll be off duty. It's for twenty-four hours."

"Have another date."

"With whom, Matthew? I don't know anyone here except maybe the man whose wife knocked him down, and she's hostile already."

"With me," I said. I'm a cat of quick decisions.

"You're thousands of miles away."

"I'll be in Athens before tomorrow night."

"No, Matthew. I've never been the sort of mother who pulls you away from your job over trifles. I know just how to handle it."

"You lure him into slipping his mitts into his own handcuffs, and—snap, snap—you spring them shut."

She giggled. It wasn't that funny. It was because she'd found a way out for herself. She was going to sign up for one of those bus tour things, a night-club tour or Athens by Night.

"A whole busload of the creatures with the little white gloves and the hairnets," she said. "How's that for a hideout?"

"Without white gloves and a hairnet of your own, you'll stand out like the one perfect digit in a double fistful of sore thumbs."

"Never," she said. "Never this side of the grave."

"See you tomorrow," I said. "And don't be so smug just because you have that beautiful hair that never does anything you don't want it to do."

"No, Matthew. I forbid it. I won't have it."

"On your own admission, you need chauffeuring, and you need patproofing. I need a vacation and a mother's care."

Of course, she rose to that. "Matthew," she gasped. "There's something wrong. You're ill. You've been hurt."

She was in the middle of rising when the line went out. That's another characteristic of the back gate to nowhere. Phone service is spotty.

I packed a bag. I wrote my son of the desert a little note. I called his attention to the clause in my contract that permitted me to take time off for rest and recuperation. I explained that a bit of important personal business had come at me suddenly. I regretted that this business was so immediate and pressing that I hadn't been able to take the time out to request an audience with the Sonof or go through any of the suitable motions of a courteous leavetaking.

I told him how much I'd always admired his interest in and

concern for his tribal problems. I praised his way of being ever ready to drop any business at hand, however expensive the interruption might be, to deal with such tribal problems. I explained that this sudden crisis that was taking me away was in the nature of a tribal problem. I reminded him that, through circumstances beyond my control, the job I was doing for him was at a standstill. I promised that I would be communicating with him long before I could be needed again, and I assured him that the little matter that was taking me away would be cleared up in short order.

Right outside the window of my little air-conditioned oasis was the airstrip. Anything that didn't come or go by ship, camel, or Cadillac, went by air; and all the air traffic landed on and took off from my doorstep. It was a good setup. Some of the plane jockeys might have been less amenable when it came to ferrying in my whiskey if they hadn't all known it would always be right there in the handiest of spots any time they dropped by to lubricate.

So with my packed bag ready at my side and my note safely stowed in my pocket, I poured myself a drink and settled down to wait. Two planes were on the strip being serviced. Soon the thirsty pilots would be scratching at my door.

My first visitor wasn't any good to me. He was going a good part of my way, to a town called Beirut, and all kinds of airliners take off from there for Athens. It could have been a breeze, but I wasn't buying it without first checking the cargo. I didn't have to probe. Before he'd even dropped the ice into his drink, my pilot buddy was telling me. He was ferrying the boss to the fleshpots, and he was licking his lips in anticipation of a little go of his own.

I said nothing. It wasn't the lift I wanted. After all, I had put some of my best prose into that note I was going to leave for the Sonof. Hitch a ride as far as Beirut with him, and I'd have to say my farewells in person. This cat hates wasting notes.

"Who else is going out tonight?" I asked.

"Guido."

"Whither bound?"

"Officially Cairo, but you know Guido."

"Who takes off first?"

"Officially me, but I doubt it."

He explained that the Sonof had only just begun briefing the spies he kept for watching his brothers. Nobody had to tell me about that. It happened every time the head man departed his realm, even if it was only for overnight. Having brothers is a thing in those parts. The biggest part of a Near Eastern monarch's job is keeping his brothers in line. Any time he takes his eye off them, he can have a palace revolution.

My Sonof never had revolutions. He'd always been free of them, whether palace or the other kind; but, as the man said, the price of this freedom was eternal vigilance. He had spies and he had a non-stop series of quiet crises.

To look at them, the brothers never did anything but play bridge and read dirty books; but they also made plots against the Sonof. The plots always got knocked off, maybe not because the Sonof's spies were that good but because the brothers made it easy for them with their habit of plotting against each other.

If you think all this is unbrotherly, try putting yourself in the place of the Sonof and his brethren. Pop, you must remember, was the Near Eastern model and he came with all the accessories, namely multiple wives and even more multiple concubines. So the brothers are mostly half brothers and each with a low idea of the maternal halves of all the others.

Each remembers mama, and that means he doesn't trust any of the others or owe any of the others anything like loyalty. But he also remembers papa, and that means he doesn't shed his brother's blood. Before, during, and after each plot, the brothers gather at the bridge table or curl up with their dirty books. The plot is knocked off and everybody goes on as always behaving like nothing happened. Only the hirelings get hurt. It's them the Sonof's bodyguards hang up by the thumbs, riddle with rifle slugs, slice up with their daggers, or just quietly garrotte. Nobody touches the brothers. It would be an offense to papa's memory,

and it would break up the bridge game. They live to plot again.
I was saying the hell with them.

Guido came by and poured himself a drink.

"Carrying any passengers to Cairo?" I asked.

"One," Guido said, "if you've got an Egyptian visa in good
working order."

"What are we waiting for?" I asked.

"Just to say *addio* to a good friend; but if good friend is coming
along, we'll just take the addio with us."

He reached for the bottle on the bar, but I brought out a new
one. We'd already had three snorts taken out of the other. You
don't shortchange a buddy who's about to do you a favor. I
brought the note out of my pocket and handed it to my other
pal.

"Mind giving that to the Sonof for me?"

He took it without even looking at it, stowed it carefully in
his shirt pocket, and buttoned the flap down over it.

"When I first see him?" he asked. "Or do I get forgetful?
And how forgetful? After we're airborne? On landing? Just before the first dancing girl? Between dancing girls?"

"Don't stick your neck out. Any time after we're off the
strip."

They thought I was flaky. I reminded them that I wasn't a
brother, only a cat the Sonof had under contract.

"Any day," Guido said, "he can start treating you like a
brother. We've seen it happen."

I laughed it off. I like Guido. I like the way he takes a plane
off the ground, and I like the way he sets one down. I like the
way he goes at life without asking anything but the important
questions. He waited with his questions until he had us off the
ground.

"Is it that you have something going for you in Cairo, *Matteo
mio*," he asked, "or just that you had nothing going for you
back there?"

"Cairo," I told him, "is just a way station."

He chuckled. "But for me, too," he said. "I carry papers to

Cairo. Two days and then I carry papers back. What do I do two days in Cairo?"

"Look at the Pyramids," I suggested. "Talk to the Sphinx."

What he told me to do with the Pyramids and the Sphinx was unprintable and also impractical. Since I had nothing going for me in Cairo, why, he asked, didn't I ride with him all the way?

"Ultimate destination?" I asked.

"*Roma*," he said. "Where else?"

"Athens," I suggested.

"You've got something going for you in Athens?"

"It's where I've got to be."

"Got to be," Guido whistled. "She'll have a friend?"

"When you have to get yours that way, it'll be the day. Nothing in Athens?"

Guido sighed. "She went into the movies. So now she lives on yachts. You know how they say about sailors? A girl in every port? That's me. I have a girl in every port, and this little Greek mama is it, and what good is that to me? I never know what port she's going to be in."

"There's the Piraeus. It's a port."

"It stinks of fish."

"You've got something going for you in Rome?" I asked.

"In Rome, but always."

So we parted at the Cairo airport. I hit the airline desks and lined myself up for the next flight out to Athens. Since there was nothing taking off before morning, the airline clerk offered to phone into town and find me a hotel room. It seemed a good idea.

There I was leaning against the counter and listening to him negotiate. I know countries where with far less discussion you could buy the hotel. My bag was sitting on the floor beside me, and along about the time it was being decided whether I would need a balcony or not, I came down with this sudden sense of loss.

You know that something-isn't-here-that-ought-to-be-here feeling. It comes over you and automatically you start taking in-

ventory. All of a sudden you're half fuzz and half suspect. You're
patting at your pockets. You're doing a self-frisk. Billfold,
change, keys, passport, watch. All present and accounted for.
Coat, shirt, pants, shoes. All intact. Buttons all buttoned. Zip-
per all zipped. So what's amiss?

Bag on the floor alongside you? Bag is not on the floor alongside you even though it was there only a moment ago. A quick
survey of the area shows up a dozen bags exactly like it. Each of
them is attached to a respectable-looking traveler. Then there's
another. I catch sight of it just as it goes whisking out the door
that leads to the taxi stands.

The gent who has this one is traveling fast. He's also wearing
a brown silk suit that has a strong purplish glimmer to it. Unless you've had experience of decayed pomegranates or Port Said
pimps, it's no good your even trying to imagine the color.

Although I didn't have anything like a clear track, I hurdled
a couple of baby buggies and circumnavigated a flotilla of stoutly
anchored grandmothers and made it out that door. A string of
taxis dozed along the cab rank. A pair of German travelers in
sweat-stained *lederhosen* and dusty red fezes were dickering
with the driver of the first cab.

No bag that looked even remotely like mine was anywhere to
be seen, no brown suit with purplish glow. I made inquiries.
The *lederhosen* had seen no one. The cab drivers had seen no
one. No brown suit, with or without purplish overtones, had
taken a cab. No man in a hurry had taken a cab, no man with
a suitcase.

I explained that it was my suitcase, and I also explained that
there wasn't a thing in the bag except my handkerchiefs and
whiskey that could possibly fit the man. I had seen the spread of
him as it disappeared through the door. On any comparison with
what he carried back there, I was a cat who had been neglect-
ing his sitting down.

Everyone was most sympathetic, but nobody was any help.
They hadn't seen him. If anything as large as that and of such

extraordinary color had come out and picked up a cab, they would certainly have seen it.

I went back inside. My friend at the airline desk had finished on the telephone. He had a room for me. They'd tried to foist off on him one without a balcony, but he had been firm. I would have the works: bathroom and balcony.

"Even a W.C.," he added triumphantly.

"Thanks," I said, and I explained about my bag.

My friend behind the counter wasted no time. "You must have the police," he said, reaching again for the telephone.

He had managed a balcony for me. The fuzz would be easy. Have you ever had police? Report a theft, and they want to know what you've had stolen. They want it inventoried. Give them a sensible answer like a stack of handkerchiefs, and right away they're climbing up your back.

"How many handkerchiefs? You don't know how many? You don't know exactly? They were your handkerchiefs? It was your bag?"

They don't say you're faking with intent to defraud the insurance company; but, after all, how can you expect them to recover your property if you don't have any competent knowledge of what's been stolen?

"If you don't get me back every last handkerchief," I said, "it'll be all right."

They assured me it would be a matter of pride with them to see that I had restored to me the bag and every last item of its contents. All the time they were talking to me, they were looking at me out of their big, brown eyes, and those big, brown eyes were so liquid with sorrow that, if I still had that stack of handkerchiefs, I could have passed them around.

They were going to put their best efforts into it, but they had to tell me that they could give me little hope. This, they explained, was Egypt, a country unsullied by crime. Egypt, however, had its eastern border, and we all knew what lay over that way.

"We must seize it before it vanishes into the east," they said.

I went shopping. I bought a razor, blades, shaving soap, a toothbrush, some toothpaste. I could also have bought a little tin Sphinx with a clock between its forepaws, but I couldn't see that I needed it. The airport shop had a stock of red fezes but no *lederhosen* to wear with them, so I decided I'd wait and replace my wardrobe in Athens.

The hotel room was as advertised. I stripped down and headed for the bathroom. I stood under the shower and enjoyed the water as it sluiced down over me. I thought of how nice it was going to be to climb into fresh socks and shorts and a fresh shirt and suit. Immediately I remembered.

I was going to have to pick up all my stuff from the floor where I'd let it fall. I was going to have to try to shake the wrinkles out of it and put it back on me. My skin crawled at the thought. It was enough to put a cat off threads for life.

I cinched a bath towel around my waist, and I pushed the bathroom door open. Looking toward the corner where I'd flung my balled-up shirt, I blinked. No shirt. I studied the middle of the rug, where I'd stood when I dropped my pants. No pants, no shorts, no socks, no shoes. I looked at the bed. No jacket.

Back home this would have been Mom picking up after sloppy old Matthew, but not here. I could smell the difference. Have you ever run onto jasmine sautéed in rancid olive oil? That was the scent, and it hung gut-wrenchingly in the air of that room. Mom never uses that much perfume; and what little she does use isn't jasmine sautéed in rancid olive oil.

II

I had a clue, didn't I? Find the party with that peculiar taste in foo juice; and you're on the way to the recovery of Erridge's stolen garments, his stolen passport, and his stolen funds. Yes, brother, it was that bad. Passport and currency were in the pockets of the missing jacket. I was down to what I stood up in—a hotel bath towel. Possessions I had left to me were the recently purchased razor, toothbrush, toothpaste, and shave cream. I'd taken those into the bathroom with me. Even the spare razor blades were gone with the threads.

I hit the telephone. An agitated assistant manager came on the run, but all he brought with him was incredulity and hair oil. While he was taking his incredulity into all the bureau drawers, under the bed, and in and out of the closet, I was concentrating on his hair oil. Sautéed jasmine, as I live and breathe, and I was getting to be a cat who wished he knew how to get along without inhalation.

He was a small assistant manager, about five feet five in elevator shoes; and, if he made as much as a hundred pounds, it would be only with the hair oil. Anything I could wear would have fitted him at least twice, but it didn't stop me thinking about him. Money doesn't come in collar sizes or chest measurements.

So we had the police. This time it was a copper quartet, and I forgot about making with the clues. That particular hair oil, I discovered, was Cairo's in thing that season. Two of the four reeked of it. The other two were as hairless as chihuahuas.

They questioned me, and they seemed to want to know what was wrong with Erridge. First the suitcase and now this. It wasn't normal for anyone to be that larceny prone. What they seemed to be trying to ask me was what purpose I had in coming into Egypt and bringing thieves with me.

It was a long session and an asphyxiating one; but finally, with assurances that none of the Cairo fuzz would sleep that night, they left me. If there was anything man could do, they would do it. By the time I was shut of them, it was resoundingly after hours, but I did get a call through to a laddie who was standing night watch at our embassy.

We explored my problem. A bit of cash could be found for me. Come morning, some credit could be lined up. Emergency replacement of my passport would take a little longer, but he would put that into the works without delay.

"You have no clothes at all?" he asked.

"Barebutt," I told him, "except for the hotel bath towel."

"Did you have any plans for tonight?"

"I've been too busy for planning."

"Then you'll be all right in your room?"

"If and when I can get it aired out."

I'd already told him about the sautéed jasmine. He even knew what the stuff was called: Lily of Luxor.

"Only because of that," he told me, "everybody wants bald-headed servants." He worried a lot about getting me some clothes. "First thing in the morning," he promised, "I'll call my haberdasher. He'll send a man around with what you need."

"Slacks, a shirt, socks, and shoes," I said.

We went over the sizes, and he assured me that at crack of dawn I'd have the essentials.

"That'll be great," I said. "Till then I'll hole up here and get what I need from room service."

"Unless the hotel catches fire," he said cheerily.

"Is it likely to?"

"With your kind of luck, brother?"

I hadn't overestimated room service. They came up with a meal and with a supply of cigarettes and whiskey. My little assistant manager lent me a book. Even though it had the smell of Lily of Luxor on it, I read it. I was even sorry I was going to have to give it back to him because I would have liked to take it on to Athens for Mom. Even though she's read everything, I was certain she'd never read that one.

My Athens plane reservation, of course, was down the hole. How do I jump borders without a passport? I read. I slept. The hotel didn't catch fire. A bald Egyptian called on me with a selection of shirts and socks and shoes and pants. He was so early that he woke me up. To this day I don't know whether that diplomat specified a bald salesman. I took it for a sign of the turning of Erridge's luck.

I ordered up some breakfast, and I was in the middle of marveling about how much better food tastes when you eat it with pants on when my ambassadorial benefactor came calling in person. He brought me a little cash loan and told me I was to be around to the embassy at ten. There were forms to fill out and such. I asked him what chance I had of making an afternoon plane out to Athens, but he gave me no encouragement. The passport thing was going to take a bit longer than that. I just had to hope Mom would make out all right without me. She hadn't told me whether her Greek fuzz was bald fuzz or fuzzy fuzz, but I was figuring they didn't use Lily of Luxor in Athens. She would have mentioned it.

It was a morning of going through the motions. There was the session at the embassy, but let's not talk about paper work. There was another conference with the police. Since the embassy was in on this one, I drew higher echelon fuzz this time around. I can report that in the upper brackets they also use hair oil, but it isn't Lily of Luxor. It's jasmine again, but uncooked.

The embassy crowd couldn't have been more sympathetic. I was invited to lunch. I was asked to a cocktail party. They consulted the calendar for that night. There was a white-tie dinner

on and two black-tie dinners. One of the younger diplomats was
assigned the job of whipping up a no-tie dinner.

Before lunch I ducked back to the hotel. The box that had my
key in it also had a flock of little white memos. The airline
had been calling me. They had been calling all the time I was
out. Would Mr. Erridge, please, call John Wiggan at the airport.

I went up to my room to make the call. I was reaching for the
phone when it rang. It was John Wiggan.

"Mr. Erridge? You won't know me by name; but yesterday,
when you lost your bag out here at the airport, I was the man on
the desk."

"Right," I said. "You made the Athens reservation for me. I
had to cancel out on that because my passport's been swiped."

"Yes, Mr. Erridge. I saw the cancellation, and the night man
told me; but the funniest thing has happened, Mr. Erridge."

"Let me guess. They've stolen the airport."

"It's even funnier than that. Your bag's back. I have it."

"You have it?"

"Ever since I came on this morning to take over my shift. As
soon as I came across the promenade toward the desk, I saw it.
Your bag exactly as you'd described it, sitting right where you
were yesterday when you missed it."

He gave me the play-by-play on it. He couldn't believe his
eyes. He went to the bag and examined it. It had my initials on
it—ME. It had my address tag chained to the handle.

"We have one afternoon flight out to Athens, Mr. Erridge. I
can get you on it."

"Without a passport, Mr. Wiggan?"

He'd been so excited about the reappearance of my bag that
he'd forgotten about my passport. He offered to send the bag to
me at the hotel, and at the risk of being late for my lunch date
I waited for it.

I read some more of the assistant manager's book while I
waited, but even the steamiest bits couldn't quite take my mind
away from wondering just what was going to be missing out of
that bag. In due time it arrived. It occurred to me that I was going

to need a locksmith. The bag had been locked, and the key was
gone with my pants.

What made me try the catch, I don't know. I put my finger on
it, and it snapped open. That surprised me so much that I didn't
even lift the lid. I just stood there staring at it and going back
through the lanes of memory. That bag had been locked when
last it had been in Erridge's possession. Also on its handle and
lid it hadn't had the brown stain that looked like dried blood.

When eventually I did raise the lid, I was again given pause.
The unmistakable effluvia of Lily of Luxor floated out of it, and
crammed in on top of what Erridge had packed in it were all
those extras, the shoes that hadn't been in the bag because
they'd been on Erridge's feet, the shirt, the socks, the shorts, the
pants, the coat, and even the necktie.

I checked the pants. My keys were in the right pocket. I
checked the jacket. My passport was where I'd last stashed it and
so was my billfold. I checked the contents of the billfold. Everything was there, money, papers, all the essentials and every last
bit of trivia.

I phoned old buddy Wiggan out at the airport and told him
the bag had been delivered complete with contents. I didn't tell
him about all the stuff that had been added. No good burdening
his mind with that. I wanted him at his clearheaded and efficient best for finding Erridge a seat on that afternoon flight out
to Athens.

"But your passport, Mr. Erridge," he demurred.

I assured him that, come check-in time, I would be complete with passport. He took my word for it. Obviously he was
thinking that Erridge rated that big with the diplomats. I let
him think it. The alternatives were too complicated and peculiar to be talked about. They might be discussed with the embassy. Beyond that I wanted embassy advice on it before I'd even
consider taking them up with the fuzz.

You see, my jacket was lying on the bed where I had dropped
it after dipping into the pockets to check for passport and billfold. As I talked to friend Wiggan, I was noticing something

about that jacket. It was lying lining-side up, and there was one seam in that lining that caught my eye. It wasn't like the other seams. It was puckered.

I'd had that jacket made for me by Brioni in Rome. If you know anything about old Brioni, you know that his seams don't pucker.

I finished with Wiggan; and before I put my call through to the embassy, I unpacked the bag and took a look at the linings of the other jackets I had in it. It showed up in all of them. The one seam in each lining was puckery, and always it was the same seam. I had a spare pair of shoes in the bag. Like everything else it contained, the shoes stank of Lily of Luxor, but the lining of the soles had another sort of smell. I checked the pair that had been swiped out of the hotel room and had now been returned with the bag. They had it, too.

Now, dig me, Charlie. I'm no teenager who goes around sniffing glue for kicks, but I do know what glue smells like. Those shoe linings had been taken out and glued back in. I called the embassy. I told them I had my passport back and everything else I'd lost. I told them thanks for everything. I said I was coming right around to thank them in person. I begged off on cocktails and dinner, explaining that I would be on the afternoon plane to Athens.

Of course, they asked how, but the call was going through the hotel switchboard.

"Little pashas have big ears," I said.

I packed everything back into the bag except the passport, money, and keys. Those I carried on me. I locked the bag, and I took it with me as I headed over to the embassy. A hotel boy wanted to carry it for me. I tipped him double for his kindness in letting me carry it myself. I wasn't about to let that bag out of my hands.

At the embassy I told all—the full account of the recovery of my possessions. I unpacked the bag for them and turned all the jackets lining-side out. I handed the shoes around and asked them to take a sniff at them.

"The linings have been out of the shoes," they said. "One seam has been ripped out in every coat."

"Meaning?" I asked.

"Meaning that somebody had reason to think or thought he had reason to think you were carrying something he wanted. It would be something you'd be likely to carry hidden in your shoes or sewn into the lining of your coat. Were you carrying anything like that?"

"No. Cross my heart. Scout's oath. All that jazz."

"Any reason for anybody to have the notion that you were?"

I suggested that this United Arab Republic might be a land of notions.

"There's another possibility," they told me.

"What's that?"

"That you now have something you didn't have before."

"Possibility?" I growled. "It's a certainty. A blood stain and the stink of Lily of Luxor."

"More than that. You're booked to Athens. Somebody wants to get something across to Athens. They put it under the lining of one of your shoes or sew it into the lining of one of your coats. You arrive in Athens, and one of two things happens. Maybe the Greek customs has an information on you. They do a complete search. They come up with something that puts you in bad trouble."

They didn't have to line out for me the other way it might go. I arrive in Athens. The Greeks give me no trouble. I breeze through customs and immigration, and then my bag is swiped again and returned to me again. I have done a job of smuggling for somebody. I thought about it, but I couldn't bring it in from left field.

"No," I said. "It isn't one suit lining ripped open and resewn or one shoe lining pulled out and glued back. It's all the jackets and all four shoes. Somebody wants to put Erridge on the spot, or somebody wants to make Erridge do some smuggling for him. He lifts the bag. He's got all he needs there for tucking his stuff away. Why does he steal my clothes out of the hotel room?"

"Your keys. The bag was locked. He needed the keys."

"And he thought I'd be carrying keys in my socks? No locksmiths in Cairo?"

They spelled it out for me. One shoe lining tampered with and one alone or one coat lining opened and resewn, and it would be a dead giveaway. I'd dig right off that something had been planted on me. It would have to be that or else that something had been planted on me back before I flew out to Cairo, and the Cairo operator knew exactly where to look for it and retrieve it.

Doing all the shoes and all the coats and going to the length of pulling off that second theft, the one out of my hotel room, brought it down to just the two possibilities. Either my Lily of Luxor thought I had something he wanted, and he had looked everywhere in my things for it, or else he had planted something on me and had done all this extra ripping and resewing and regluing to con me into thinking he had been looking to take something out and not to put something in.

"So," I asked, "you think something has been planted on me?"

They suggested having the police in to search my stuff. I objected.

"Hand them something as fancy as this," I said, "and how fast will they move? Will I be on that Athens plane this afternoon?"

"Not a chance."

"Then no fuzz, Charlie."

"It's not that easy. They're looking for your missing passport. You turn up at the airport to check out of the country. You show your passport. They'll want to know where you got it."

"I ride on the Wiggan hypothesis. Some jerk picked up my bag in mistake for his. He returned it."

"Your passport was stolen out of your room. They know that."

"All I have to do is tell them Erridge is the kind of dim bulb who, instead of stowing his passport away in his pocket, puts it in his suitcase. He's so dim that he forgets what he's done and thinks it's gone with his coat even though he had it in the bag all the time."

Officially they couldn't approve it. Unofficially they could pick no holes in it. So officially it went down that Erridge told them he'd been wrong about where he'd had his passport. Happy, happy news. It came back in his bag.

Taking a coat apiece we ripped out the stretches of puckery sewing. Nothing inside. We pulled the shoe linings. Nothing under them. The glue was still so fresh that all we had to do was push the linings back in. They held. The seams were something else again. I was all for taking off with them ripped out. I'd get them sewn in Athens.

"Not to worry," said the embassy cats.   C637393

Sewing, they told me, is in the domain of the distaff side. My problem would be put in the hands of the embassy wives. We went to lunch, and my repacked suitcase went with us. My host put the bag in the hands of my hostess. She needed only the barest briefing. Me and his colleagues he led to the bar. Drinks were whipped up for the lot of us. My host knew what the distaff side would be drinking; and at the first clink of the ice, we were joined by my hostess accompanied by the wives plus one extra, a sister-in-law assigned to see to the happiness of old Matthew. Each of these babes had one Erridge jacket; and since there were more babes than jackets, one of the wives and the sister-in-law had found a couple of socks that needed darning. They sewed as they drank. When I suggested that I was putting them to a lot of trouble, they agreed sweetly that I was. But didn't men always?

The departure for Athens was VIP. I was taken to the airport in an embassy car. Two of the embassy lads came along, and so did the embassy sister-in-law. She was all right. She almost made me want to stay on in Cairo. Checking out of the country went easily enough. The fuzz were there, but they were troublesome only in a minor way. I told them my story, and they snapped at it so eagerly that it was plain they were happy to have me out of the country. I could bug the Greeks for a change.

III

When the plane took off, I sniffed for Lily of Luxor and looked
for a brown suit with the purplish overtones. No dice. The
Egyptians on the plane who had hair used the other kind of hair
oil, the one that smelled like uncooked jasmine. There were a
couple who were the right shape for the purple-brown suit, something more exaggerated in its spread than a pear, more like a
butternut squash; but they were both hairless. I watched them
for a while, but I got bored with it. That particular shape, after
all, is endemic all around the eastern rim of the Mediterranean
and on down through the Arabian peninsula.

The big news on the flight was a Mediterranean sunset that
fell on some mountains that stuck up out of Crete and set them
to looking as though alchemy had it made. By the time we were
putting down at the Athens airport, night was falling. You know
what it's like coming into Greece on a U.S. passport? First it's
like coming off a plane anywhere. You wait for the ground crew
to get around to disembarking your luggage. Then you wait some
more. First you wait for the man who is going to stamp your
passport without looking at it. He's resting or something. Next
you wait for the cat who'll put you through your customs in-
spection without ever looking at your luggage. He's also resting.
All in all, it adds up to a goodly spell of waiting time.

I waited, and eventually they turned up. Stamp and stamp.
Erridge was whisked into the country. It was dark by then, and
the moon was up. In most places the road in from the airport

takes you past all the places you never see in the travel folders, but the Athens deal is different.

That road in from the airport is travel-folder all the way. First it's a string of beaches, and even in the dark they look good. Moonlight on the water, moonlight on the beach umbrellas. Then, as you come into town, your road does a long curve around the foot of the Acropolis. Up there sits the Parthenon, and if the earth hadn't spawned its moon before that baby was built, it would have had to kick off that shiny satellite then, because obviously that's what the moon is for, to touch those columns with the light they deserve.

You'll probably not take much notice of the Jupiter temple as you go by it, but it's there. When your airline bus finally deposits you in Syntagma Square, it parks to the left and you debark to the right. Traffic's snarling around you. You're snarling right back at it.

Although it's full dark by then, I'm not too much worried about Mom's affectionate fuzz. The look of all that traffic is reassuring. It's going-home-from-work stuff. I recognized Athens as one of those towns where the night life doesn't get away to any early starts. I figure it will be a little later before Mom's police pal will be showing up for his date. By my calculations this'll be about the time when he'll be changing out of his uniform, curling his mustaches, and limbering up his patting paw.

I hail a cab and say Achilles. The cabbie looks interested but uncomprehending. I try again.

"Hotel," I say. "Achilles Hotel."

No dice. I start running through languages.

"*Albergo* Achilles. *Gasthof* Achilles."

A fellow-passenger I hadn't noticed on the plane was standing at the curb beside me. I had noticed him on the bus coming in from the airport, and I guessed he'd come off some other flight, probably a local deal since he was without luggage. He was helpful.

"Achilles," he said to the cabbie.

I'll admit he didn't say it the way I did. He put a touch of gargle onto the CH, but to me it didn't sound like such an over-whelming difference. The cabbie, however, lit up as though the moon had strayed off the Parthenon to shine on him.

"Achilles," he said. "Nay nay."

I was about to try for another cab jockey, one that wouldn't have his invisible OFF DUTY sign up, when I remembered something Mom said about her troubles with the language. "Nay" was yes, and "okay" was no.

I thanked my benefactor and made to climb into the cab. He said it was his pleasure, and he patted me. Where? As Mom put it, where do they pat you? So whose pleasure was that?

I swung around and, without even knowing I was doing it, I was making fists. Meanwhile, however, he moved off. He was picking up his own cab. I heard him say Achilles again, and that cabbie, who was standing at the curb, patted him as he went in.

Now that maybe figured. This cat had shiny, thick, black curls falling down over his forehead. He had big, brown eyes. He had the kind of mouth he could make do with for talking and eating and such, but it was obvious that none of those was the mouth's primary purpose. He was in his early twenties and built like a fencer. You know, light, graceful, wiry strong, like a trigger spring or a coiled snake.

I shrugged it off, unclenched, and finished climbing into my own cab. We were fighting traffic all the way, and the two cabs crawled along shoulder to shoulder. Every time I looked in that direction, my young friend would catch my eye and make with the smile. It should have been a good smile, the kind that would make you trust him if only because he had all those beautiful, little white teeth. Can there be anything wrong with a young man who so obviously has never forgotten to brush his teeth after every meal? There can. Don't ask me how I knew, but somehow I did. Somehow that smile didn't work. It made him look like an angel gone bad.

I tried staring him down, but it did no good. He just met me eye to eye and smiled the harder. So I was a stranger in town and

I looked around at the sights. We were driving along the edge
of a park, and there were flower stalls all along the park wall.
The flowers were tulips, and they were the best thing I'd looked
at since the Parthenon. They looked the way tulips look, as
though they had no problem, and why should you?

After a while we ran out of park and flower stalls, and that
meant that the tulips stopped. I read street signs, or I tried to.
Some of the letters I knew because they looked like letters anywhere. Some others I could dig because they turn up in mathe-
matical formulae, and you don't get to be an engineer without
having looked at those. Pi and Sigma and Lambda were within
the Erridge ken, but mostly they didn't put together to carry any
meaning for me even when a word didn't come up with some
letter I'd never seen anywhere before.

Reading street signs you don't dig must lie pretty low in anybody's gamut of fun things to do, but the main idea was to look
anywhere but in the direction of that cab that all the way was
hanging alongside. I told myself to cool it, not to be a square,
all that jazz; but I just couldn't talk myself into it. That smiling
elf in the other cab had me bugged.

We ran through a neighborhood of new apartment houses
with rows of little cast concrete balconies all over the front of
them. I was thinking you can overdo balconies. Get them that
numerous and close together, and you're doing nobody any good
unless it's a second-story man.

We went up a long curve of a broad driveway and hove to in
front of a snazzy dazzle of marble and glass. The name of the
place was carved in the marble, but it was as rough as any of
the street signs. Two words, and the first one I didn't even try
to dig. It began with one of those letters I didn't know at all,
and it went on and on and on. Even the easy ones had been giving me trouble. I wasn't ready to try tangling with any thousand-
drachma word. I worked at the second word. It read: "Axilles."

My cabbie put one paw on the door handle, and with the
other he pointed at the taximeter. I read him loud and clear.

He wasn't opening the door for me. He was making sure I didn't open it until I had paid him off.

"Achilles?" I asked, putting everything I had into gargling the CH. It should have been enough. I felt a tonsil tug at its moorings.

"Nay," the cabbie said, and left off pointing at the meter to wave toward all those letters carved in the marble.

I waved toward them, too, and reached back for that Greek lesson Mom had given me over the phone.

"Axilles, okay," I said. "Achilles, nay."

The smile turned up in the cab window.

"This is it," he said.

"Go away," I growled.

"I'm trying to help," he said, putting more and more intimacy into that smile. "This is it. You're at the Achilles."

"Axilles," I snarled.

He reached in the open window, took me by the chin, and started turning my head toward the right. I chopped the edge of my palm against his wrist. He took his hand back and checked out the hookup he had between hand and arm. It was obvious that he was trying to dig how it could look all right even when it was feeling like a freshly amputated stump. All sorts of things seemed to be happening to his face, but none of them touched that smile of his. It stayed fixed on me, leading a life of its own.

Out of the corner of my eye I caught the marble facing at the other side of the broad entrance. There was a name carved over there, too. The smile had been trying to turn me toward it. I read it.

"Hotel Achilles," it said, in Roman letters.

I wanted to apologize. Honestly, I did. After all, I am a friendly sort, and I've never been known to bite a helping hand, but this whole thing had me bugged. Even the simplest of apologies was going to lead to further misunderstandings. No good could come of it.

I paid the cabbie what the meter was asking for and tossed a tip on top of it. The boy with the smile jumped forward to

snatch the money out of the cabbie's hand; and even though that
cab jockey's fist closed down on those drachmas as quick and as
hard as a bear trap, it was obvious that the smile would have
been in there even quicker if his wrist action'd had a little more
time for coming back to normal.

He put the smile away and scowled at the cabbie. They were
so busy jabbering at each other that for a while they forgot me.
The cabbie was still holding the door shut, and this other baby
was leaning in the window. It began to look as though Erridge
was in that cab for the rest of the night unless he did it the
Athenian way and disembarked on the other side, out into the
traffic.

The doorman came forward, and the cabbie let go of the door
handle. I turned it and pushed gently. I wanted out, but I wasn't
ready to get rough about it, not that soon after I'd been that
wrong. The push was enough. Pretty boy fetched up the smile,
put it back on his face, and revved it up to full power, as he
turned back to me.

"In Athens," he said, "you never tip cab drivers."

"Thanks," I said. "I won't do it again."

"That thief should have given it back to you."

"You ask too much," I said. "And thanks for showing me
the sign I could read. I shouldn't have chopped you. I'm sorry."

I was coming out of the cab as I was saying it, and the apology
was the mistake I thought it was going to be.

"It's all right," he said. "My hand's as good as it ever was."

Maybe he was demonstrating and maybe he just wanted to be
reassuring. Whichever, need I tell you? He patted me again.
Meanwhile the doorman is standing by. He reaches past me and
brings my bag out of the cab. I'm forgetting just long enough
to let him take it. Right off I remember, and I'm ignoring everything else, while I put all I've got into keeping my eye on that
bag.

"The rest of it in the trunk, sir?" the doorman asks.

"That's all there is," I say.

Now that doorman is wearing the correctly deadpan look,

but behind it there's something growing. It isn't a smirk. It's the strain of keeping the smirk from showing.

"The gentlemen have a reservation?" he asks.

Mostly when a foreigner talks English you can't be too sure about the finer shades of pronunciation. You can't pick him up on the difference between gentlemen and gentleman. You can't even make anything of the difference between have and has. Greek's rough on me. Why shouldn't English be rough on them?

That's one way of looking at it, and I'm trying to look at it that way, but I have my doubts. I've had too much experience with hotel people in foreign parts. Anybody who's traveled will tell you the same thing. It's a booby trap. Such English as they speak, they speak impeccably. It's so good that you think they'll dig what you say, and they do but only as long as you stick to the script. Say something that's even the least little bit off the line of their standard routine, and you lose them.

Now this question about reservations is right down the middle of any hotel doorman's routine. It's no good assuming that it's just his English coming apart. It's what he's thinking. Two guests with one bag between them, that smile, and that pat. He's putting two and two together, and he's coming up with a sum that makes him want to smirk. So what can Erridge do beyond wishing that maybe the doorman's control will break down, and the smirk will leak through on to his puss, giving Erridge a reason for belting him in the mouth?

My self-appointed buddy digs it the way I do. "We are not together," he says. Then he turns to me. "You have a reservation, of course?" he says.

"I don't," I say.

"I'm afraid . . ." The doorman begins making like he's about to flag me a fresh cab.

"Let me do the worrying," I tell him.

I'm right about the English. I've said something that isn't in the script. He doesn't dig it. My young friend says something to him in Greek. It has the right effect. The doorman leads us to the revolving doors. Inside he sets my bag down. I pick it up.

"Leave it, sir," he says. "A boy will take it." It's the perfect English again.

"I carry my own. I'm peculiar that way," I say, as I hand him a tip.

He's looking baffled. Even "peculiar" is beyond him.

Again he gets it in Greek, and he looks a little less baffled. Maybe now he digs the language, but he doesn't dig me.

"If they have a room for me," I say, "send the boy around. I'll tip him for letting me carry my own bag."

My young friend chuckles and talks some more Greek. Coming back into English, he explains. "I told him it isn't you're tight-fisted," he says. "I told him you even tip cab drivers."

So he's reaching for me again. So I pivot away from it. I put my hand out to shake.

"Thanks for everything," I say. "I'll be all right now."

He shakes, but, when I let go, he doesn't. "They may be full up," he says.

"If they're full, they'll find me something somewhere."

"They can't always do it."

He moved his hand up to my elbow and, taking a firm grip, started me toward the reservations desk.

Short of slugging him, there seemed to be no way I was going to be able to shake loose from him, and I wasn't giving myself any guarantees that even handing him a snootful of knuckles would do it. There was something about this baby that suggested that he might very likely enjoy being slugged.

That's a big lobby they have there in the Axilles. The walk from door to desk isn't done in any stride or two. For all the space, furthermore, it's no place for stepping out. It's populated, but heavily; and damned if all the dames don't have the hairnets and the little white gloves on. There are far more dames than guys, but such males as these babes have in tow go along with Mom's story. Every last one of them looks as though he'll take only the slightest bump—something like a nudge perhaps—and he'll go down.

So they're not immovable objects. That's not meaning you go

plowing straight across, bowling them over to right and left. You thread your way through. You move in and out. You go around them. About halfway across the lobby my pal lets go of my arm and waves me toward the desk.

"There it is," he says. "You can see it from here."

It was a change of tune. There'd never been any suggestion that he had to stay with me so I wouldn't get lost in the Axilles lobby. The idea had been that he had to be handy in case they didn't have a room for me, and I'd need him for finding me another hotel.

Now I've got no less curiosity in me than the next cat, but I was settling for it this way. I'd keep my curiosity and lose my guide.

So he faded. He put the smile away and replaced it with the look of a man who's just remembered that when he parked he left his motor running. He had important business elsewhere, and he had to be off tending to it in a hurry. He was so much in a hurry that he left me without in parting even giving me another of those little pats.

I bellied up to the desk and asked for Mrs. Erridge's room number. If I'd leaned across the counter and spit in the clerk's eye, he couldn't have looked more put out, but that wasn't the whole of it. There was this gent who had just been coming away from the counter.

You must get the picture. He'd finished his business with the clerk, and he was pulling out of there in such a hurry that he wheeled around and was taking off without even looking where he was going. Only because I was looking and because I'm okay in the footwork department, we missed out on a collision; but now I ask for Mrs. Erridge. My request is obviously mildewing the clerk's yoghurt, but I can't put my mind on him because this other gent charges back in even a greater hurry; and along the whole broad, unpopulated expanse of that shiny, marble counter he can't find any place to stand except so close to me that I can feel his breath blowing through my hair.

Now, I don't have to go on tippy-toes to make my six-one.

Standing at my altitude, I've had people breathing down my neck; but, not moving in basketball circles, I couldn't remember ever before having anybody breathing down on the top of my head.

This was one big man, daddyo. It wasn't just that he went up through the timberline. He was a Hercules; or, giving him his Greek handle, a Heracles. Over in Sicily there's an old Greek temple that, instead of using columns, is held up by something they call Atlantes, naked male figures, strong, thick columns of marble muscle. This bucko was one of those with clothes on. He was of an age where he could have started running to fat, but not this one. There was the silver in his black curly hair, and there were the lines in his face, but he was putting his weight on me, and even through his clothes and mine I could feel it. He was just like his brothers on that Sicilian temple, a big, thick column of muscle and as hard and heavy as marble, except this baby was made of hot marble.

I let him have the elbow, but it didn't move him. I edged off a bit along the counter. If Heracles followed along to go on crowding me, I'd obviously have to deal with it, but I wasn't looking for it. He didn't follow along. He just stood there.

The clerk looked at me. Heracles looked at me. The clerk looked at Heracles, and he didn't like what he saw. He turned back to me.

"Mrs. Erridge has checked out," he said.

"She left a forwarding address?"

"If you leave a message for her, sir, we'll forward it."

"I'm her son. She was expecting me. Didn't she leave a message?"

"No, sir. She didn't."

"How do you know?"

He looked pained. "I'll look for a message, sir," he said. He rummaged around for a while under the counter, but he was keeping an eye on me all the time, as though he was looking for me to steal the X out of Axilles. After a while he came back to me. "Sorry, sir. No message, sir."

"She did leave a forwarding address?"

"I'll look, sir."

He went to look, and came up with a card. He let me look at it. I'd asked for a forwarding address, and I had a forwarding address—Bayardstown, New Jersey, U.S.A., the house I was born in, and he even had the zip code on it.

It wasn't impossible. Mom could have grabbed a plane for home, but it wasn't like her. Mom's no quitter.

"You can do better than that," I said.

I drew a blank from the clerk. Patiently I tried to explain it to him. I was her son. I knew that address. I wanted to know where I could find her right now, where she had gone when she checked out of the Axilles.

The clerk sighed. He excused himself. He promised to return in a moment. Would I, please, wait?

"I'll wait," I growled, "but don't be long."

Heracles came and leaned his weight on me again. "Go away and forget the whole thing," he said.

"Who the hell are you?"

"Be smart. You don't want to know who I am."

The odds were lousy, but this had gone to where I couldn't stop to figure odds. I pulled back, looking for swinging room. He moved right along with me, right down to the end of the counter. I fetched up against a column, and I had no place to go. I had a column pushing into me from either side. Both felt like marble. One was without muscles and one with. One was cold. The other wasn't.

I worked at setting myself to do something useful. He felt me setting myself, and I could feel how he was setting himself to meet my move. In case I wasn't digging it, he put it into words.

"I give *karate* lessons," he said. "If you know how and the other man doesn't, you can do a lot with it; but if both of you know how, it's like any fighting. A good big man always gives a good little man a licking."

Nobody had ever called me a little man before, and the "good" didn't pull any sting out of it.

"You're big," I conceded. "You don't have to prove anything."

"If I turn you loose now," he said, "will you just go and not come back? Go and take your friend with you?"

He was losing me. "What friend?"

"Kostya. You're keeping him waiting."

"Who the hell's Kostya?"

"Every time I look over there, he dodges around the corner."

I looked back over my shoulder. It was my self-appointed guide sticking his head out from behind a column. Our eyes met, and he broke out that smile again; but now, along with everything else it was, it was nervous. Heracles made a small move. He was crowded in so close against me that he couldn't blink without me feeling it; but even if I hadn't felt it, I would have known. The smile dodged back behind its column.

"Get lost, the both of you," Heracles said again.

"The hell with Kostya," I said, "and the hell with you."

Heracles sighed. "I want to be nice," he said plaintively.

The clerk came back and took up where we'd left off.

"The day clerk might know more about where Mrs. Erridge has gone," he said. "I don't think he will, but you can come back tomorrow and try."

"I can also go to the police," I said.

"That might be a good idea, sir," the clerk said.

Heracles eased off enough to give me room to come out of my corner. I picked up my bag and walked away from them. I didn't look around to see whether Heracles was following, but I could guess that he was coming along behind me. The bucko he called Kostya dodged around his column and didn't show again.

I went out and picked up the doorman. I told him to get me a cab and to tell the cabbie to take me to the American embassy. The doorman whistled a cab off the rank, but by the time it had pulled up, Heracles was alongside me. He had something in his hand that looked like a short string of big beads. They were cylindrical, about an inch wide and an inch thick, and they were loosely strung on a heavy nylon thread that looped around and fastened with a green tassel. The beads were pale yellow, an amber color, but they weren't amber—some sort of tough plastic. All the time we stood there, Heracles played with his beads, running them back and forth on the nylon cord, clicking them one against the other.

The doorman ushered me into the cab, and he spoke to the cabbie. I caught one word that sounded enough like American to be reassuring, but I wondered whether it took all those other words to say embassy. The doorman shut the cab door, and we took off.

"American embassy," I said, trying to make sure.

"Okeydoke," said the cabbie. "American embassy it is, mister."

English it was, and purest Weehawken. He'd hardly taken off before we hit a red light, and I dug what started the idea of seat belts. Stomp a brake the way that baby did, and you better have everything tied down tight. Erridge wasn't tied down at all. Erridge was leaning way forward, talking to the driver, and his center of gravity was no place it ought to have been. Erridge fetched up against the back of the driver's seat, and a couple of Roman candles went off inside his eyeballs.

He shook the lights out of his eyes. He explored for cracked ribs while he worked at sucking some air back into his lungs. He started to scramble back on the seat, but he didn't have to bother. He had all the help he needed. Heracles was sharing his cab. He still had those beads, but now he had them wrapped tight around his knuckles.

I stuck my head out of the window and yelled for a cop. None in sight. Heracles dropped a paw on my shoulder and hauled me back in.

I didn't expect it to do much good, but I aimed for the most vulnerable spot within reach and jabbed hard. It did no good. The big cat rolled away from it. Pinning me in the corner of the cab seat, he brought up the hand that had the beads wrapped around it. Slowly and thoughtfully he massaged my jaw with those beads. I wondered why he thought he had to make so sure

I got the idea. So they were updated brass knuckles. So this was the modern thing, made of plastic.

The cab was doing a U-turn when he found the spot he wanted. If he drew his hand back more than four inches before he exploded it back in, Erridge is no judge of distance.

IV

Yellow plastic did everything brass could have done. Old Matt went sleepy-by. The Weehawken-talking cabbie brought him out of it. Cold water drips on the face. The eyes flutter open. I'm lying on my back on what feels like a flat stretch of gravel. Looming up above me is what looks like the underside of a bird-bath. It's overflowing slightly. There's grass near-by and flowers and shrubs. There's also the cab driver. He's standing by the bird-bath, pushing water out of it down on to Erridge.

"After you've rolled a man," I ask, "don't you take off?"

"You ain't been rolled, mister."

"What have I been?"

"It was a mistake. He said for me to tell you he's sorry. He said for me to take you to your mama."

"Stop with the water," I snarl. "It's for the birds."

He gives up on the water and bends down to me. Hooking his ankle with my foot, I snick it out from under him. The slack of his pants smacks the gravel.

"I was only going to help you up," he says.

"I don't need any help."

"All right. Climb in the cab. I'll take you to her."

"I'm taking you to the nearest cop."

"Where you going to find one who talks English?"

"I show him my jaw. I turn out my pockets."

"Turn them out. Go ahead. You ain't been rolled."

I got to my feet. He made to get to his. Planting a foot in his chest, I set him back down again. I went through my pockets. Passport, billfold, money, everything, all there.

I sighed. This was getting monotonous. "So it's the suitcase," I growled. "My stuff won't fit him."

"The suitcase is in the cab. Nobody touched your suitcase." I didn't believe him. "We'll go see," I said.

He was in no hurry to move. "All right if I get up?" he asked.

"But behave yourself. One funny move, and I'll take you apart, and without those plastic knuckle-dusters either."

"Worry beads," he said. "They're good for the nerves."

I explored the swollen and tender area along my jaw. "Didn't do mine any good," I said.

We were in a park. The thing I'd taken for a bird bath was a drinking fountain. It was up a little graveled alley off a path. The alley was flanked with shrubbery and arched over with trees. The air was loaded with jasmine, but this wasn't hair oil. This was fresh and pure. Looking down the alley, I could see the cab where it stood parked in the roadway. I headed for it. The cabbie followed after me. With every step he took on that gravel, he crunched audibly. He was keeping his distance. He was more wary of me than I was of him.

My bag stood on the cab floor just where I remembered setting it down. I unlocked it and lifted the lid. It looked just as it had when I'd last seen the inside of it at the Cairo airport. I wasn't about to unpack it for any more thorough check. That could be done in the police station. I shut down the lid and turned the key in the locks. Something had to be going with that bag. I was being super-careful with it till I could find out what.

So there I am, bent over with my head inside the cab, and I'm being super-careful; and then it happens again. The old, familiar pat in the old, familiar place, and the old, familiar voice.

"Let's go, my friend," says the old familiar voice. "I've fixed the driver. He won't be bothering us."

I back out of the cab fast, and I wheel around. It's Kostya again. He's got the smile back on, and he's got it juiced up to its fullest strength. He's also in the process of unwinding one of

those strings of beads from around his knuckles. His beads are
red, and they have a white tassel, but otherwise they're the same.

"Where'd you come from?" I ask.

"Taxi," he says. "I have it waiting by the park entrance."

"Where's my cabbie gone?"

"He'll sleep a while. We can be far away before the big one
comes back. That big one, he's bad."

Kostya's afraid, and with every passing second his fear is growing on him. I can smell it. I grab me a handful of Kostya.

"Where is the cabbie?" I snarl.

"We don't have time to go screwing around with him."

I hit him, but just the flat of my hand square across the smile.
"Where is he?"

He points. He's needing his tongue for counting up his teeth.

I pop around behind the cab and have a look. The cabbie's flat
on his face on the road. It's a hard-surfaced road, and that's why
I didn't hear him go down. On the gravel he would have made a
most noticeable crunch.

I roll the man over. His eyelids have begun to flutter, and his
lips are working. Kostya comes up beside me.

"You have a handkerchief?" I ask.

"You haven't time to blow his nose for him."

"Soak your handkerchief and bring it back to me."

"That's not what he needs. I've got what he needs."

He's wrapping those beads around his knuckles again. I'm
developing a strong prejudice against those beads. My prejudice
against Kostya is like a good wine. It's improving with age.

I take hold of his arm, and I go to work on it. You don't have
to rip the arm out of its socket. You don't even have to break it.
You can make any man feel that he's got an arm he never needed.
Kostya whimpers. The pain doubles him over. Those beads, that
are good for the nerves, fall out of his nerveless hand. I pick
them up. Easing off on his arm a little, I rub his face down with
his own beads. Maybe even I forget for a little that it's only
Kostya's face I'm kneading. I tell myself that maybe some day
I'll get a chance at Heracles. This is good practice.

Then I turn him around to put his patting area in range. Letting go of him, I swing my foot. The kick catches him just as he's falling. It straightens him up and sends him flying. You'll think I'm putting you on, but you should have seen it. If Kostya had been a football, he would have split the goal posts right down the middle.

That does it. As soon as he gets his feet back under him, he takes off and goes scuttling up the road. I can hear a hum of traffic in that direction, and I can see moving lights through the trees. He's headed for that park entrance where he said he left his cab. I would like to take off after him. He, too, could be examined in the police station, but I have to make choices. I have to stay with my bag. It has the longer history of giving Erridge trouble.

My cabbie has his eyes open, but he doesn't want to go anywhere. He's asking me how he's going to drive with all those spots in front of his eyes. He says jockeying an Athens hack is one hell of a way to make a drachma. It's bad enough without passengers beating up on him.

I'm not apologizing for anything or explaining anything. He'd been no help to me when I was up against Heracles. I wasn't forgetting that. I tell him he's going to drive me around to the police station. He says he's dizzy. He doesn't know when those spots before his eyes will go away. He thinks maybe they'll never go away. He's in no condition to drive.

"I'll drive," I say.

"You don't know where."

"You'll tell me where."

He agrees, and I'm asking myself what's wrong with me. He's going along with everything I tell him. So what more do I want? I want him to look less happy about it. We get back into the cab. I take the driver's seat, and I have him beside me. He hands me his cap.

"What's that for?"

"You put it on. The first corner we hit outside the park,

there'll be a policeman. He sees you driving without a cap. He'll stop us."

"And take us to the police station where we want to go anyhow."

"You wanted to go to your mama."

"You know where she is?"

"Go where I tell you. You'll see. I know."

"How do you know?"

"I just know."

"I just don't believe you. Police station. Which way?"

He tells me to drive on straight ahead. I drive out of the park, and he's reasoning with me. I'm all right. I can see. I have no spots in front of my eyes. I haven't been robbed. I've lost nothing. What have I got to complain about? If anybody has a complaint, he's the one. He has those spots. He's describing them to me, spot by spot, when we come out of the park and hit the first intersection.

It's as he said. The fuzz on traffic duty thumbs me to the curb and strolls over. As he strolls, he's bringing out his little, black book. I try him in English. He has no English. I run through all the languages I have. He hasn't any of those either.

He brings his hand up in the stop signal and turns to my hackie. With him the fuzz can communicate. And do they? Back and forth, back and forth. Another cop, who's just patrolling, comes over. They kick it around among the three of them. I try my languages on him. He hasn't any of them either. I bring out my passport. Even if they can't read it, they might recognize the U.S. seal and dig up an interpreter for me.

The passport does have an effect. Both of the cops make a study of it. They like it. It galvanizes them into action.

With all kinds of polite little bows and kindly smiles they give me back my passport. The patrolling officer motions me out of the cab. He holds the door to the back seat open for me. He slides in behind the wheel. The other one goes back to the middle of the street. The light is against us, but he plays it big. He stops traffic and sends us on through.

It's only a short drive, but interesting. This can't be Mom's fuzzy boy friend. Mom had distinctly said her boy was going to be off duty and out of uniform. It has to be that they all drive like that. Hell bent for disaster, the way Icarus flew the time his pop gave him wings.

We skirted the park till it came to an end at a big building with *evzones* standing guard around it and beyond it a huge square thickly planted with pepper trees. Turning away from the *evzones* and the square, we nosed into a broad avenue where the traffic bucked and eddied like a stew pot in need of watching. Any minute that whole maelstrom was going to start climbing up the fronts of the buildings and spilling out across their roofs like a pot boiling over.

My cab whizzed to the curb. "Here we are," said the cabbie.

The fuzz made "here we are" gestures.

"Police station?" I asked.

"Your mama," said the cabbie.

"Mama," the cop shouted happily.

It was the one word we had in common. I checked on it later. Greek and English, same word, same pronunciation. If you're going to Greece, and you can get by without talking about anything else, Charlie, you're in.

There were signs on the marquee at which we were standing. I couldn't do anything with the Greek one, but I dug the other. It was in English.

"Queen's Palace Hotel."

The doorman opened the door for me. I sat tight.

"Do you speak English?" I asked.

"But naturally, sir."

"Great. Would you just naturally tell the police officer driving this hack that I want the police station and an English-speaking police officer to whom I can make a complaint?"

I'd done it again, departed from the script. The doorman began looking as though I'd kicked him square in the middle of his welcoming smile. He turned to the front seat for clarification. Of what they told him, I could dig only two words that kept recurring. They were "Erridge" and "Mama."

The doorman came back to me, but only to say "moment, please" before he scooted back into the hotel. I made use of the moment. I copied the number off the hack medallion. I leaned forward between the cabbie and the fuzz. I was looking for the officer's shield number. Seeing me with my address book and pen, he was right in there digging me. He turned in his seat and held his shield so the light would hit it.

The doorman came back with another character, obviously the hotel manager. Nobody dresses like that any more except for getting married or for managing a hotel. He didn't look like he was getting married.

He was putting down the welcome mat. He was rolling out the red carpet. He was unleashing at me the full long-lost-brother treatment.

"Mr. Erridge, we've been expecting you, sir. Honored to have you with us, Mr. Erridge, sir. You had a good journey, I hope, sir. Your mama will be so happy. She did keep saying she hoped you wouldn't come, but we all know how our dear mamas are, God bless them."

"Maybe I haven't come," I said ungraciously. "First I want a police station. After that maybe I'll be back."

The manager leaned into the cab, put his lips against my ear, and whispered. "Are you being wise?" he asked. "After all, Mr. Erridge, isn't it the last thing your dear, dear mama would want you to do? Didn't she come to us from the Achilles only because she was trying to avoid the police? I know we are being selfish about this, but the Achilles's disaster has been our good fortune. When a lovely lady like your mama favors us with her patronage, we just cannot lose her to some other, inferior hotel; and if the police come bothering her here, we will. Please, Mr. Erridge. Please, sir."

I had the shield number. I had the medallion number. I had a case of confusion I thought maybe Mom would know how to clear up. Maybe I would be smart just to quit. At least I could wait till I could pick it up again with an interpreter of my own.

The manager was so happy about getting me out of the cab and into his hotel that he couldn't work up much grief even over my insistence on carrying my own bag. He whisked me straight into the elevator without stopping at the desk for registering or any of that jazz. The treatment was strictly red-carpet, but when I found myself alone in the elevator with this manager, and he brought a string of those beads out of his pocket and started clicking them, I came down with the feeling that it might be a red-carpet kidnaping.

I had some beads of my own, the ones I'd taken away from Kostya. I had only the manager's word for it that he was taking me to a room Mom had reserved for me. It was obvious that I'd hit this Queen's Palace only because it was the place where that hackie had been dead set on taking me. It was also obvious that somebody had put the idea in the hackie's head. Heracles? Kostya? It would have been nice to think I was going to find Mom upstairs, but I was warning myself against going wishful. It seemed more likely it would be someone else.

Just to suggest to this manager that Erridge not only knew how to handle himself but had even picked up some pointers on handling himself the Greek way, I brought Kostya's beads out of my pocket and wrapped them around the knuckles of my right hand.

The manager grinned. "Worry beads, Mr. Erridge?" he said.

"I picked them up on my way to the hotel. What do you use yours for?"

He shrugged. "Same as everybody else," he said. "You run them through your fingers. It soothes the nerves."

"That all?"

"Better than tranquilizers."

"Quicker anyhow."

From the look of him, he didn't dig that. The elevator stopped at the twelfth floor. A room-service waiter with an empty tray was just coming out of the room opposite. He saw us and left the door ajar. The manager asked him a question. It was Greek again, and it contained neither of the words I'd been recognizing, not mama and not Erridge.

The waiter answered by nodding upwards. Considering all the trouble I was having with the language, it will probably astonish you that I was hep to the gestures. This nodding up bit isn't confined to Greece. Greek shopkeepers spread all over the eastern Mediterranean and even farther afield. Wherever they are, they speak the language of the country, but their gestures stay Greek. This nodding up is like our shaking our heads. It means no.

The way you do it is you raise your eyebrows. Raise them so emphatically that they carry your head up along with them. You can say okay, and nine times out of ten they won't believe you mean no. It's probably because you can't quite believe it yourself. You've got to be a born Greek speaker to say okay and make it sound properly noish. It's not because you don't give it the right pronunciation either. It's because you can never quite get it out of your head that okay is an affirmative sort of sound. Haul your head up by the eyebrows, and they'll dig you fine. That's no.

The way the manager scowled, it was obvious that he didn't like this no. Since he worked up a smile for me and bowed me toward that open door, I didn't like it either. That room was occupied. I could hear someone moving around in there. If Erridge is going to have roommates, he wants to do the picking.

I caught him in midbow. "My room?" I asked.

"Yes, Mr. Erridge. It's one of our choice rooms, sir. Nowhere in Athens will you find a better view of the Acropolis."

"Who's in my room?" I asked. What I was hearing in there wasn't the view of the Acropolis.

"It's only the maid," he said. "She's putting fresh towels in your bathroom. She won't be more than a moment."

I set my bag down and checked on my plastic knuckle-dusters.

"I'll wait here till she comes out," I said.

"She should have been done in there long ago," the manager fretted.

He darted through the open door and barked an order. He got an answer barked right back at him. When the barking's human, it's no trick at all to tell dog-bark from bitch-bark. What was coming back at him was bitch-bark, no mistaking it.

They came out of the room together, and the Greek they were throwing back and forth was all snap and snarl and crackle. I've since been told it's another hunk of the well-known Glory that was Greece come on down into modern times along with the Acropolis. The classical word for it is the *agon*, and it goes all the way back to Socrates and before. It's a knockdown and dragout argument, and there's nothing a proper Greek loves more.

As chambermaids go, this was an uncommonly beautiful one. Hers, however, was the Greek kind of beauty. They call it calipygian, but if you're too tired to go to the dictionary, take my word for it—it's service weight. Getting a load of Erridge, this great, big, beautiful *baklava*—honey cake to you—lunged for my bag.

Our mitts hit the handle together. She hauled at it, and I hauled back. Since it was only a step or two from the hall to the room, we had it on the luggage rack before we'd torn it in two, but nobody's going to say we didn't try. Having fought me to a draw on the bag, she now took a grip on my coat. She seemed to be asking whether I was going to give it to her or would she have to rip it off my back.

The manager shouldered her off me; and, while he explained things to me, she kept circling us like a wrestler looking for a hold.

"Your suit, Mr. Erridge, sir," he said, "needs attention. You look as though you'd been in an accident, sir."

"I'll ring for valet service," I told him.

He turned to her and translated. She appealed to me. She also reached, and the way she kept reaching, it was obvious that if she wasn't watched, she would strip me not only of my coat but of my shirt and pants as well.

Erridge found himself beginning to learn the language. It seems like the Greeks had language before they had clothes. The words they use for pants and shirts and stuff like that aren't their own. They've swiped them from the Italians, and Italian Erridge digs.

She was asking me if it could be true that I didn't want her to strip me naked right then so she could go off with my threads and put them in shape for me. I didn't have the words for telling her that, when a babe strips Erridge naked, it isn't for valet service, so I raised my eyebrows and let them haul my head up after them. That did it. She accepted a tip and withdrew. The manager bowed out after her.

I shut the door and bolted it. Standing with my back planted against the bolted door, I looked my room over. It was a large room with a picture window. Outside the window was a balcony of the sort I had noticed from my taxi.

Beyond the balcony sat the Acropolis. I suppose at that moment it was beautiful, too; but I can remember looking at it then and not thinking about beauty at all. I was thinking that it looked strong and honest and decent. It looked as though, when the Greeks put the Parthenon on it, they'd put everything to rights forever. A cat, looking at it, could trap himself into thinking nothing could be devious or hidden or wrong. He was in a world that knew no liars or thieves or cutthroats.

I took my coat off and looked at the back of it. It called the Parthenon a liar. Like an old maid out of a comic strip I peered under the bed, looked in the closets, explored the bathroom. Like a CIA agent out of a spy thriller, I wrapped my cellophane cloak around me and looked behind all the pictures, examined all the lamps, lifted the mattress, and checked the telephone. If the place had been bugged, it was no obvious job.

I picked up the phone to listen for that proverbial click. The situation called for it. At least they could be monitoring my phone calls. The operator came on, and I detected no extra click.

"*Kalispera*, Mr. Erridge," she said. "Good evening."

It sounded friendly, but I was in a mood to call it too friendly. "What does *kalispera* mean?"

"Good evening, Mr. Erridge."

"You already said that."

"I did, sir," she explained. "In both languages."

So Erridge learned a little more Greek. It's *kalimera* by day and *kalispera* by night.

"Do you have any messages for me?"

"No," she said. "No messages, Mr. Erridge."

I was about to hang up, but she said the desk wanted to talk to me. They came on, but they had no messages either. All they wanted was my passport number. They were sending a boy up with the registration card. They were just about blubbering with grief at putting me to so much trouble, but would I do them the great, big, fat favor of filling it out and sending it back down with the boy? Maybe it was the red-carpet treatment, but I was off balance for it. It was too big and too sudden a switch after the Axilles.

I looked at my room some more. It was a luxury-type room. Everything in it that wasn't a rich, juicy brown was a rich, creamy tan. The bathroom was more of the same. It was all marble, brown marble veined in tan. If chocolate almond bars turn you on, it would be for you, Charlie.

Even the pictures behind which I'd found no bugs were sepia prints. Any other time I would have been content to pour myself a drink and settle down to look at my pictures. They were great, big, beautiful photographs of great, big, beautiful marble babes. If you are visualizing what they used to have hanging in the schoolrooms back when you went to school, the Winged Victory or even the Venus de Milo, then you haven't even begun to dig the Glory that was Greece.

I had two pictures in that room. One I liked a lot. The babe in that one was bending over to tie her sandal. She wasn't nude, but what she had on looked like the thinnest and most transparent chiffon. In addition to being that thin and that transparent, it looked as though it was soaking wet. It clung to her all over, and in the important places it clung closest. Find yourself the most luscious sex-kitten available. Get her into a half ounce of see-through nightgown and dunk her in the swimming pool. You dig me? Whooee!

The babe in my other picture you have to see to believe her. I

had her only from the waist up; but, Charlie, that was enough.
She had no clothes on at all unless you're going to count a crown
of snakes that sat on top of her head. Between the snakes and
her shoulders she was beautiful. From the shoulders on down
she was excessive. Breasts, brother. She had them in rows, in
layers, in platoons. Take them two by two, and they were as
good as the finest pair you've seen anywhere; but the cat that
sculped her knew a place where he could get them for her whole-
sale.

I began to wonder whether I needed that drink I thought
I needed, or if possibly I'd already had it. Drink, they say, can
make a man see double. Me? It's never hit me that way, but
there can always be a first time, except that this wasn't anything
as tame as double. Squared didn't even make it. She was mamma-
lian to the nth power.

Reeling back from the impact of the art of ancient Greece, I
went into automatic action. On the bedside table sat everything
I needed. There was a bottle of whiskey, a couple of bottles of
water, a bucket of ice cubes, and a bottle opener. Hardly looking at what I was doing, I stripped the foil from the top of the
whiskey bottle, pulled the cork, and poured myself a slug—re-
storative size. I dropped a couple of ice cubes into it; and, prying
the cap off one of the water bottles, I splashed in the habitual
small dollop of water. I raised my glass to the babe in the wet
chiffon, since I was drinking to the other one only with my eyes.
Before I could bring it back to my lips, I was interrupted by one
of those discreet knocks. I set the drink down, picked up my
worry beads, and wrapped them around my knuckles before I
went to the door. It was only a bellhop. He'd brought up the
registration card for me to fill out. Actually I didn't even have
that much to do. It was just read it and sign it. Everything else
had already been done for me. Name—Matthew Erridge. Per-
manent address—Bayardstown, N.J., U.S.A. Business or profes-
sion: Engineer. Purpose of Visit: Pleasure. Arriving from: The
back gate to nowhere (not that way, of course, but by its atlas
and gazetteer name).

I signed the card. The bellhop and I exchanged *kalisperas,* and he took off. Bolting the door after him, I told myself that this was just a little something more that needed thinking about, and I returned to my drink. Raising it again toward the wet tomato, this time I did bring it to lip-reach. Taking a long, anticipatory breath, I filled my nostrils with the aroma of that whiskey, and I lost my appetite for it.

Nothing could have been more familiar than that aroma. I held the glass up to the light and shook it a bit. Never a bubble. I set the glass down and checked the bottle. It was my brand. I looked at the water bottles. They were uncharged water.

So it wasn't to drink. It was also to think about. Step by step, I went over the way I had come to this hotel. That taxi driver had brought me. He had been determined to deliver me here and nowhere else. Then there'd been the welcome I had in the hotel. I'd been expected. They'd known all about me, all the info they'd put on the registration card, exactly what kind of whiskey I favored and more than that—they even knew that I didn't like it loused up with any bubbly water.

"What you don't dig, Erridge," I told myself, "you don't drink. Not tonight, you don't."

So it was thought-provoking, but it didn't seem too serious. The thirsty traveler would just move on to another oasis. I had a bottle of the same in my bag, and that was a bottle I knew about. It was mine. It had been tested. Guido and I'd had a snort apiece out of it en route to Cairo. I got as far as lifting the lid of the bag, but the stain on the leather reminded me. We'd checked everything, but we hadn't given the whiskey even the first thought, and the seal of that bottle had been broken before it passed through the hands of the Lily of Luxor.

The weary traveler was going to have to struggle on to yet another oasis. First, however, he had to have a switch on the threads. Could that chambermaid be stopped a second time? If this soiled and rumpled Erridge again came within reach, she was a cinch to snatch him barebutt.

I washed up a bit and changed my pants, shirt, and coat. I'd done a complete check on the room, the closets, the balcony, the whole bit, but there was one door I'd been ignoring. Like the door to the hall it had a bolt on it, but it wasn't on the right wall for leading out to the hall, and its lock was a far simpler type. The lock didn't matter much since on the other side of the door there would also be a bolt. Both bolts have to be drawn back before the door can be opened. In other words, the occupants of the rooms on either side of such a door must be agreed on wanting connecting rooms.

While I was changing, the thought came to me that this was the hotel where everything was provided even before I got around to asking for it. Just in case, I took a good look at the door. The bolt on my side of it was in the pulled-back position. My hosts had set me up in a hospitable stance. Erridge was expecting visitors.

Before I tried the doorknob, I picked up my worry beads again. I was growing real fond of those beads. If anyone had asked me to name the greatest accomplishments of the Hellenes, I would have said the Parthenon and worry beads. Just in that one evening they had become a part of me.

Properly armed, I turned the knob. On perfectly oiled hinges the door swung toward me, revealing the blank face of a second door. I admired the set up. I hadn't expected anything that im pregnable.

I wanted to know about that room next door. I went out to my balcony. Every room had one, all the way up and down, each linked to the next straight across the front. If the architect had taken on the job of creating the most scalable of all possible walls, he couldn't have done better unless he installed elevators clear across the face of the building. Climbing up hand-over-hand from balcony to balcony would be only a little more difficult than walking upstairs. Stepping over the parapet from one balcony to the next wasn't difficult at all.

I stepped over. The glass doors to the room next door stood open. The room was dark. Telling myself that I was putting far too much reliance on my worry beads, I went in. The moon shining in helped me locate the lamp that stood nearest to hand. There were heavy draperies and I pulled them across the window. It shut out the moonlight, but I had a good fix on the lamp. I could reach it in the dark without falling over anything.

I switched it on and looked around me. It was another brown and tan room, very little different from mine, and it was Mom's room. I recognized her luggage. I recognized her monogram on the luggage. The perfume that hung in the air I recognized for hers. I knew it well. Every time I come home to Bayardstown, I bring her a jug of it. I also recognized the picture she had set up on the dressing table. It was her boy Matthew all done up in his first tuxedo.

Maybe she'd brought it along because she hadn't known what the Queen's Palace was going to do for her in the way of pictures. This room of hers also had two sepia prints, but hers were the other sex and nothing taking any fig-leaf cover. It made me wonder whether the hotel was split up that way into boys' rooms and girls' rooms or if the chambermaid changed the pictures along with the towels.

I checked the bolt on Mom's connecting door. It was like mine, drawn back out of the socket. I left it alone. Switching off the light, I drew the draperies back. I returned to my own room by way of the hall. I was heading for that drink I had poured out and not used. Since it was Mom who had the room next door, the whiskey was less suspect. She knew my preference in drink the way I knew her preference in foo.

I looked at the glass, but I didn't touch it. I still had too many unanswered questions. So Mom's things were in the room next door. She wasn't there. It was still not so late that she couldn't have been out on the town either with her pat-prone policeman or hiding from him, but her boy Matthew wanted to see her. He wanted a satisfactory story of how she had left the Axilles and how she had come to the Queen's Palace.

If this considerable hunk of man could have been shanghaied into this chocolate almond bar of a room, what said that his little, defenseless Mom could not have been similarly shanghaied? As far as I knew, she didn't even have a set of worry beads to wrap around her knucks.

I went out on the balcony and looked down into the boil of traffic below. I looked up and down the street. Maybe I was hoping to see some green lanterns, though what was to say they do it that way in Athens, marking their fuzz pads with the pair of green lamps?

Anyhow I didn't see any, but across the street and a little further along was a sidewalk cafe. It had the fashionable look. It might have been imported from Paris or Rome. It looked sad, homesick for the Via Veneto or the Rue Royale.

No cafe anywhere could have so much the Parisian or Roman look and not have waiters who spoke, if not English, some other language Erridge digs.

I headed downstairs. I met nobody in the hall and all the way down I had the self-service elevator to myself. On the way through the lobby I made another try at the desk. Were they quite certain that Mrs. Erridge had left no message for Mr. Erridge? They were quite certain.

"When did you last see Mrs. Erridge?"

"This evening, sir, when she went out."

"She didn't say where she was going?"

"The Athens-By-Night tour."

"She told you that? She was alone?"

She'd had the desk reserve her a place on the tour. The hall porter had escorted her across the street himself, and he had put her on the bus. It figured. The bus would load across the street. This side its doors would have been along the curb, and the company would have had to answer to the Unhellenic Activities Committee.

"How long do these tours last?"

They would be returning within the hour, possibly even within the half hour. It all depended on the traffic in the Plaka.

"You understand, sir. It's the old section, a big bus, narrow, twisting streets."

"The other guests who went on the tour, were they wearing hairnets and little white gloves?"

"Please, Mr. Erridge?"

"Never mind."

I headed for the street. The hall porter came after me. He had his worry beads out, and he was clicking them. I watched him closely. If he so much as started to wrap them around his knuckles, Erridge was going to take him. He didn't wrap them.

"Would you like to leave a message for Mrs. Erridge when she comes in, sir?" he asked.

"I'm not going far," I said. "I'll see her when she gets back."

I crossed the street to the cafe. I had my choice of tables. I took one in the front rank where I had an excellent view. It covered both the hotel entrance and the curb across from it where that Athens-By-Night bus could be expected to disgorge Mom right into the middle of what had to be the worst whirlpool of traffic in all Athens.

The tables stood row on row in front of the cafe, but maybe five of them were in use, and the patrons had scattered themselves as widely as possible. I was the only one who had chosen a front-row seat.

Between my table and the curb I had no want of company. There were newsboys. There were shoeshine boys. There were strollers. There were also the seedy diplomats. I counted at least a half dozen of those. They ranged in age from the twenties to the fifties, but they all had the same briskly important manner. They were all a bit down-at-the-heel, a bit frayed-at-the-elbow, and a bit five-o'clock-shadowy; but they all carried the leather attaché cases.

That one of them had picked me for his own was obvious. He didn't approach me, but he paced back and forth in front of me and his eye was steadily on me. A waiter came out of the cafe to take my order. I had been looking at too much untouchable whiskey back there in the hotel room. Suddenly I seemed put off the stuff. I decided I'd go native with *ouzoo*. The service was quick. In no time at all my waiter was back with the tall glass with the couple of inches of clear, colorless liquid in it. He set it down in front of me and flourished a water bottle. I watched it turn whitish where the water hit it. It looked like Pernod. It smelled like Pernod. I took a sip. It tasted like Pernod, but only if you've been drinking in a bar where they make their own. The waiter went back into the cafe. Immediately the diplomat, who had picked me for his own, zipped over. He said nothing, but as he went by, he dropped something on my table—five toasted hazel nuts. They looked good, but I left them alone. Erridge was remembering his schooling. Latin. Virgil. "*Timeo Danaos et dona ferentes.*" I fear the Greeks even when they bring gifts. I could tell myself that I wasn't afraid of anyone. Let them come. I'd meet them worry bead for worry bead. But I hadn't drunk their unsolicited booze. I wasn't eating their unsolicited nuts. The waiter came back.

"You don't like nuts?" he asked.

"I didn't order nuts."

"Those are samples. They always give out samples."

"They?"

"The fellows with the brief cases. He'll be back soon to sell you a bag of nuts. That's what they carry in the brief cases."

"And the diplomatic pouch? It travels in a nut basket?"

The waiter laughed. He picked up one of the sample nuts and popped it into his mouth. I waited for him to wash it down with a slug of my ouzoo. He didn't. I ate a nut. They were even better than they looked. I ate the rest of them. I sent the waiter off for another *ouzoo*.

While he was gone, the diplomat returned. This time he opened his attaché case and, bringing out three bags of nuts, he set them on the table. Three sizes—small, medium, and large. Pointing to each bag in turn, he gave me fingers to count up for the price. The large one was fifteen drachmas. I picked it up and handed him twenty. He put the change in my hand and with it a white card.

Then whisking the small and medium bags off the table, he darted away. I watched him as far as the corner. There, with a frightened look tossed back over his shoulder, he took to his heels.

I turned the white card over and read it. The lettering had a Greek sort of shape to it, but it was English and no trouble at all.

"*Matt,*" it read. "*We must talk. The big one is not your friend, and he is not through with you. I know how men look when he is through with them, and it must never come to you to look like that. He's watching you right now. Stay in your room tonight. I will come to you there. Listen for me. I will knock five times, a pause, and then three more. Open your door to no other knock.*"

There was no signature.

V

When the waiter arrived with my second drink, I engaged him in chitchat. I picked up my sack of nuts.

"My man," I said, "sold me these and took off."

"He doesn't figure you'll want any more right away."

"They're good. I could use some more to take back to the hotel."

The waiter looked around for the nut peddler. He shouted a question at one of the man's confreres. The question was relayed down the line from attaché case to attaché case. None of them knew anything.

The waiter shrugged and turned back to me. "He'll be around," he said. "They go to the cheaper back-street cafes when they want a drink or maybe for the gents. He'll be around."

I sucked on my second *ouzoo*. I nibbled at my hazelnuts. I read and reread my note. Obviously I wasn't digging it, but was that new? I could hardly remember when I'd last drawn anything but blanks. I couldn't let that bug me. I had a more immediate problem—Mom. Any minute now that Athens-By-Night gandergig would be pulling up. If Mom was not aboard, I would hail me a cab and have the cafe waiter tell the hackie to take me around to police headquarters. It would then be a matter for the top fuzz, the embassy, and maybe NATO and the UN.

But suppose Mom would be aboard that bus. Suppose she had come to the Queen's Palace quite of her own accord. Was Er-

ridge ready to tell her how he got there? He would be up in that
room in the Queen's Palace. She would be in the connecting
room. Did Erridge want to sit around with her waiting for
that fancy knock to come at his door? When it did come, who
could it be but Kostya? Kostya or an unknown, and Erridge was
not about to introduce either to his one and only mother.

I beckoned the waiter and asked him for my check. That was
easy, but he was worried about those toasted nuts I needed. The
peddler should have been back long since. Even if he had the
bladder of Poseidon, the sea god, he wouldn't have needed this
long in the gents.

"They're always going around the corner for a fix," the waiter
said, "but they come right back."

That put the lid on it. I just couldn't have Mom meeting any
friend who picked up junkies to carry his anonymous notes for
him. So how, without scaring her, was I going to persuade her at
that time of night to pack up and move to another hotel? Better
still, how was I going to persuade her to make the move without
even stopping long enough to pack up?

As I crossed back to the Queen's Palace, I was studying on
that. The hall porter came out from behind his desk.

"Mr. Erridge, sir," he said. "Did your friend find you?"

"What friend?"

The hall porter looked desolate. "Then he didn't find you."

"A Greek friend?" I said. "He asked for me. He got my room
number. He phoned up to the room, but I wasn't there."

I was after the answer to one of my questions—how my
anonymous buddy was going to know at which door to knock
five times and then three.

"No, sir, Mr. Erridge," the hall porter said. "The man was a
foreigner."

"American."

"No, sir, not an American, but a foreigner."

So Kostya maybe wasn't Greek. I described him. If I had
turned purple with orange pustules, the hall porter couldn't have
looked more startled or worried.

"Mr. Leonidas?" he muttered.

"Kostya Leonidas?"

"Yes," he said. "Constantine Leonidas. He checked in a little while ago, but he didn't ask for you or anything."

"He checked in, but somebody else was looking for me."

"Yes, the foreigner."

I'm told the ancient Greek word for foreigner was "barbarian." He didn't use the word, but he did make it sound as though he was thinking "barbarian." He described the man. The bushy, black mustache meant nothing to me. The bandaged left hand meant nothing, the bushy, black eyebrows.

"I don't know what nationality. Egyptian or Syrian or Lebanese. I think Egyptian, but only because of the pomade he had on his hair."

I picked it up. "French-fried jasmine," I said. "Brown suit with a sort of purplish shine to it. Balance a pear on top of a couple of fat legs, and you've got the man's build."

"I told him you hadn't gone far, sir," the hall porter said, "but he wanted to see you right away. He went out to look for you."

"And Leonidas checked in. Before the Egyptian asked or after?"

"After, sir."

"What room's he in?"

The hall porter went to the desk and checked. He came back to me with the room number. It was on the floor above mine.

I looked at my watch. "That Athens-By-Night tour should be back by now," I said.

The hall porter checked his own watch. "Any time now, sir, during the next half hour," he told me. "In the Plaka a driver can be lucky with the traffic or he can be unlucky."

At the back of the lobby was a bar of the visibility-zero type, romantically dark. A headwaiter picked me up at the bar door.

"I want to set up a party," I said.

"Yes, sir. Very good, sir. My pleasure to serve you, sir."

"Got any champagne?"

"But certainly, sir. Would you like the French?"

I liked the French. He was to ice it. If the lady came before I returned, the hall porter would bring her in. The headwaiter was to look after her till I came back.

"My pleasure, sir."

I thought maybe I ought to tell him not to enjoy himself too much, but I skipped it. He was a waiter, after all. He wasn't fuzz. Returning to the lobby, I blinked in the glare of the lights and gave the hall porter his instructions.

I had to go upstairs for a little. If the Plaka traffic was bad enough, I might be back down before the bus pulled in. Meanwhile the hall porter was to keep a sharp eye out for Mom.

He gave me his guarantee that he would be standing by to help Mom down from the bus step. She would cross the avenue on his arm. He would be watching over her. She would come to no harm.

I let him see a neat little bundle of drachmas I had at the ready, and I gave him a message for Mom. I had arranged a welcoming party for her in the bar. She was to go right in there and settle down. Under no circumstances was she to go upstairs. I didn't want us missing each other. She was to wait for me in the bar.

"The bar man knows about it," I said. "He's expecting her."

"Yes, Mr. Erridge," the hall porter said. "Very good, sir. Thank you very much, sir. In the bar, sir."

I popped into the elevator and pushed the button for my floor. As the car started up, I could see the hall porter, the desk clerk, the manager, and the headwaiter out of the bar. They were all watching the indicator. Not a man in that lobby who didn't feel he had to know whether Erridge was going up to his own room or to Kostya's.

I left the car on my floor, and I used the stairs for my ascent to the next. I found the room. Kostya also had a view of the Acropolis. He wasn't directly above either Mom or me, but he wasn't too far from it. Just a couple of rooms over to the right.

I gave his door the knuckle. No answer. I gave it the whole fist. No answer. I banged the worry beads against it. No answer. I tried the trick knock—five and a pause and then three. No answer. I took out my pocket address book, and I ripped a blank page out of it.

"Mr. Leonidas," I wrote. "He was a Spartan, wasn't he? I always thought the kid who just stood there and let the wolf chaw the guts out of him wasn't all that brave. He was just stupid. So maybe that's the way it flakes for all Spartans. I could easily have broken your arm, stupid, or your neck. I didn't because I didn't want to. If you come anywhere near my room, I will want to. You can either just go away and stop bothering me, or you can take your chances. If, when you get this, you still have any ideas about me, any ideas at all, you can call my room and I'll come up and listen to what you have to say. Maybe you can talk me out of doing anything to you, maybe not. That's the chance you'll be taking; but if you come knocking at my door or you come anywhere near it, you'll never get to talk at all. That's a promise, and it goes for you, for your bigbutt Cairo buddy in the brown suit, for your nut peddling messenger, and for anybody else you might think of sending. Sincerely yours, Matthew Erridge."

I slipped the note under the door as far as I could make it go. An edge of the white paper was left showing on the hall side. I trotted down the hall as far as the stairway. Looking back from there, I couldn't see that edge of white paper any more. I tiptoed back to check. It wasn't showing. The note had been pulled in. I waited a couple of minutes. He might be a slow reader. He might need a little time for digesting the message. Nothing from the other side of the door but silence. I gave it a repeat on the trick knock—five, pause, three. Silence.

I trotted down the stairs. I was hoping it meant that he had changed his mind about wanting to see me or talk to me, but it might just as easily have meant that he wasn't alone in there, and he didn't want me seeing who he had with him. There were all sorts of possibilities, even the one I didn't want to think about at all, and that was Erridge was too late for keeping this thing away from Mom because Mom had already been in it before her boy, Matthew, touched down at Athens airport.

Down the one flight, I made for the elevator. The indicator showed that it had just started up from the lobby. I hit the button and waited. The car sailed on past me to stop at the floor above. I kept my finger on the button. It came down the one floor and opened up for me. I stepped in and hit the lobby button.

As the door closed on me, I smelled it. Automatically I hit the button marked "14." Athens is like any place. It's not that they don't have thirteenth floors. It's just that they call them "14" in the hope they'll be lucky. For all I know it was the Greeks who started that nonsense. They had them the Furies, and the Furies scared the pants off any right-thinking Greek. So they called them the Eumenides in the hope they would be. Eumenides, I'm told, means the gracious goddesses. Is that calling thirteen fourteen or isn't it?

The relays on that elevator weren't built to take a change of orders. I had committed myself to the lobby, and it was taking me down to the lobby. I had every intention of riding it back up again. I liked the idea of meeting Kostya and brown suit when they would be together.

I come to the lobby, and the door opens. Who's there waiting? Mom, of course. The hall porter is with her, and he's working hard at talking her over to the bar, and it's evident that he isn't making it. His relief at the sight of me is pathetic. Mom spots me, too, and it makes her happy, but hers is a pale joy alongside the hall porter's, and I'm not even his son.

Mom looks wonderful, and that's one load off Erridge's mind. All thoughts of going right back up to fourteen are put away because obviously I'm not taking Mom up there with me.

She looks me over while I'm looking her over, and everybody's happy. We're both in good shape. I grab her and give her the big kiss. She breaks out of it after a little to introduce me to a dame who's been there all the time. The dame and the hall porter are hovering around our edges.

It's a Mrs. Grymm. She's taller than Mom, and she's heavier, and she looks a lot older, which can mean something or not, because if there's ever been a dame who doesn't look her age, it's Mom. Grymm's wearing something that makes her look as though somebody just raked up all the autumn leaves from one helluva big lawn. It's all layers on layers of ovalish flaps of brown chiffon, fluttering with her every breath. She has these chiffon flaps like the titmouse upstairs has breasts or the hotel has balconies. Her hair is white, and her face and arms are red. She's wearing the hairnet and the little, white gloves. The way she stands and moves, you know she was captain of the field hockey team maybe fifty years back, and she's never gotten over it.

She sticks one of the white gloves out for me to shake. The way she's built, I'm expecting one of those hearty, pumping deals you can use for jacking up a trailer truck, but I get the limp and boneless bit instead.

"Martha Grymm," she says. "It's spelled with a Y and two Ms, even though I look like an I and one M, and don't deny it, young man, because I'm the one with the right to be telling the fairy tales."

Her voice is like a flute played by somebody who doesn't know how to blow. There's very little of it. It sounds as though it's always on the edge of slipping right out of audibility. It's sweet and shrill and breathy, and it doesn't stay on key. The words go with the babe's looks. The voice goes with the handshake.

You couldn't give her any arguments. Any way you spelled her, she was grim. Granted that I'm prejudiced, but looking at Mom alongside this formidable hunk of stuff, I wondered a little how Mom gets by without a lot more patting coming her way. Not that Mom ever needed this kind of contrast to make her look good. She's always been shaped. She's always known how to dress. She never looks as though she's put any effort into it, more like a dame who just can't help looking great.

It's really not so remarkable, come to think of it. We Erridges are famous for our taste in women; and it was Pop, after all, who picked her; and nobody's ever been more Erridge than Pop. So let's face it. Mom has looks; and, boy, has she kept them? I come all over proud looking at her.

"What's all this about a party in the bar?" Mom asks. "Champagne?"

"What else? First drink with my pet parent."

"I told them to put whiskey in your room. Didn't they?"

"I didn't know you drank whiskey with men in hotel rooms."

"I haven't been," Mom concedes, but she takes a doubtful look toward the black hole of the bar door. "I haven't been in there either," she says.

"Why not? Afraid of the dark?"

She twinkles at me and turns to Grymm. "You'll join us," she says.

"You don't need me now," says Grymm, sort of heading for the bar anyhow. "You'll want to be alone with your son."

"We'll need help with all that champagne," Mom insists. "I don't know whether Matt should have any. He's reeking of *ouzoo*."

"I drink it for the hazelnuts," I explain.

"How did you get to this place?" I ask over the champagne. "I was looking for you at the Axilles."

So then I have to be set straight on how X isn't X because it's something else they call Chi, like in Sweetheart of Sigma, of course, and therefore it's Achilles.

"I was looking for you there," I say.

"And so was that policeman with the hands," Grymm puts in. "We didn't know whether you or he would turn up first, so we moved over here and didn't tell the Achilles desk where we were going."

"The fuzz been patting you, too, Mrs. Grymm?" I say.

"There was a time," she says, "but even then it was only in Greece and that was years ago. Now not even in Greece."

"Mrs. Grymm suggested this place," Mom explains, "and it's a find, Matthew. The people couldn't be sweeter. It costs far less than it does over at the Achilles, and it's nicer in every way."

"And how was little old Matt going to find you," I ask, "with the desk back at the Axilles not knowing where you went?"

"The way you did find me, silly," Mom says airily.

"You fixed all that up for me?" I ask, knowing full well she didn't, but just putting it astride a dolphin to see if it would get off at Delos.

Mom isn't taking all the credit. She's scoring her brown-edged buddy, Mrs. Grymm, with an assist. The idea had been to get away from any place where the amorous fuzz might find her. Change hotels and leave no new Athens address. That's for Pattypaws. For Matthew a note is left, sealed and addressed to him. The desk is told that her son is arriving. They are to satisfy themselves that the gentleman is her son, and they are to give him the note. The note furnishes name and address of the Queen's Palace in both English and Greek. The Greek is to show to cab drivers in case of difficulty.

Mrs. Grymm's contribution was checking the spelling of the Greek part of the note because Mrs. Grymm has the language right where she wants it. Mom struggles with it, but Mrs. Grymm is a whizz at it.

"They don't pat Mrs. Grymm," she says, "because Mrs. Grymm knows exactly how to handle them. It's not only knowing just the things to say to them to make them behave. She also knows all their little tricks."

Through Mom's praise of Grymm I get to dig all the little fasties they put into that note that somehow never came into Erridge's hands. Even having acquired Mrs. Grymm as a protectress and with Matthew about to come swooping in to share in mounting the defenses, Mom still prefers to dodge the embarrassment of being followed over to the Queen's Palace by the pawing *polizei*.

Erridge will get the note. He will go out front and climb into a cab. He will ask the hackie to take him to the Queen's Palace Hotel. Doesn't the doorman hear? Won't the doorman pass the word on to other interested gentlemen? If the desk can be pressured by the fuzz, why not the doorman? Their own departure will be no problem. Grymm knows the way to the Queen's Palace. Mom just has to get up the nerve to drive again.

It has to be fixed so Matthew won't give it away. Mrs.

Grymm is the one who has that figured. Tell him to get a cab. Tell him to tell the doorman he wants to go back out to the airport. Once he's away from the Axilles, he shows the hackie the Greek address in the note. That's it.

They're so pleased with themselves, I'm not the cat to tell them it didn't work. Anyhow I can't tell them without going into exactly how I did find them; and the one thing I'm working on the most is not opening up that pot of yoghurt.

From where the ladies sit, everything's explained. It's a closed episode. From where I sit, I can see out into the lobby. The hall porter keeps turning up outside the bar door. He keeps looking in, and there's something that seems meaningful in the way he looks. I have the feeling that he's trying to catch my eye. Since my eye is lost in the dark, he can't see it, but he keeps trying.

While the waiter is pouring the last of the fizz, I excuse myself and tell the ladies I'll be right back. As soon as the hall porter sees me coming, he moves off a little. It's all too clear. He's not going away. He's just setting up our huddle in a part of the lobby where we'll not be under the surveillance of anyone in the bar, like Erridge's mama, for instance, and Erridge's mama's friend.

"Something stirring?" I ask.

"The foreigner came back while you were upstairs."

"Yes, I know."

"Then you saw him?"

"No. I just smelled him in the elevator when I took it back down."

"I didn't know whether you'd want it mentioned before the ladies."

"Right. I don't want it mentioned before the ladies."

I went back into the bar, and the three of us polished off the champagne. When we started upstairs, the ladies needed their keys, and I picked them up at the desk for them. We had the three rooms all in a row, and I wondered whether that was by deliberate arrangement. Mom to the right of my room, Grymm to the right of Mom. Mom neatly sandwiched between her two protectors.

I thought back to the door arrangements in my room and Mom's and recognized happily that they didn't connect all the way across the row of rooms, only in pairs. Grymm wouldn't be en suite with us, and I liked that. I had nothing against the babe, but I wasn't ready to take her into the family.

Going up in the elevator, I noticed that a good deal of the Lily of Luxor had faded out of the air in the car, but not all of it. More than a memory lingered on. Mrs. Grymm commented on it.

"What sort of a hussy would drench herself with this horrible stuff?" she asked.

We saw Mrs. Grymm to her door, and then I took Mom to hers. I went into the room with her. The chambermaid had been around since last I'd been in there. Mom's slippers were set by the bedside, and a nightgown had been laid out on the bed.

The Greeks are talented. They have sculpture in their blood. That nightgown wasn't just laid there. It was arranged. The skirt was spread. The waist was pinched in. The bosom part was inflated. How she puffed them out that way without a bicycle pump I'll never know.

Maybe it's because Erridge has an engineer's interest in methods. Maybe I was just bemused with imagining how Mom would look if she was shaped that way. Maybe it was because I got to thinking of Grymm's nightgown given that treatment, but I never noticed that the connecting doors between Mom's room and mine had been set ajar until Mom had gone through into my room and was calling me from there. She sounded startled and a little worried. My first thought was Kostya. It couldn't have been brown suit in there because I would have smelled him.

I zipped in after her, and it wasn't anybody. I relaxed. I thought of the obvious. It was that picture of the titmouse, but Mom wasn't giving her even as much as a glance. She was stand-

ing over my bedside table, looking at the stuff that stood on it.
She was worried.

"Matthew," she said. "Please don't feel that I'm nagging you,
but I wish you'd tell me what's wrong?"

I did a quick survey. The bloodstain on my bag didn't show
up that much; and anyhow, unless you were in the know, it
didn't look like blood. Also she wasn't looking at the bag. She
was completely intent on the stuff on the bedside table.

"What's wrong with what?" I said with more caution than
wit.

"What's wrong with you? You're full of *ouzoo*. You fix yourself a drink up here, and you insist on champagne downstairs."
She picked up the glass. "What was this for? Did you have to
have it all ready for you in case the champagne and the *ouzoo*
wore off while we were coming up from the bar?"

"I didn't drink it," I said. "You can see I didn't drink it."

"But Matthew . . ."

"Have you noticed the pictures in this room?"

She gave them a quick glance. "The Wingless Victory fixing
her sandal, it's from the balustrade of the Nike Apteros temple.
The other's one of those wild Artemis things. They show an
oriental influence," she said, and she was just talking off the top
of her mind while underneath she was hanging on to her worry.
"And you accuse me of changing the subject."

"Waiting for my luggage at the airport," I said. "I had an
ouzoo. Then at the Axilles, reading that complicated note of
yours, I went into the bar and had another *ouzoo*."

"The Achilles bar," she said firmly, "is no lighter than the one
here. You couldn't read a thing in there unless it was Braille."

"Okay, Grand Inquisitress. I read it in the lobby and digested
it in the bar. Then here they told me you're out on the belly-
dancer route."

"There are no belly dancers. There are waiters who sing *Never
on Sunday* while the food gets cold, and the olive oil congeals all
over it, and there are dancing bartenders who seem to be in a
Charleston contest at a Navajo rain ceremony."

"Maybe the night life was better back in the time of the Oriental Artemis," I ventured.

"Never mind the Oriental Artemis. There are pictures in my room, too. We're talking about your drinking."

"The part I was coming to when you changed the subject, darling, was my not drinking," I said. "They tell me you'll be back soon, and in a flush of filial joy I order the champagne. Then I come up here, and that Oriental Artemis just about knocks me over. Completely bemused by the titmouse, I act automatically. I'm not even thinking about what I'm doing. I fix myself that drink, but I get it up under my nose and I come to my senses. I ask myself does whiskey go good with *ouzoo*, and I remember the champagne downstairs. I put the drink down and I never touch it. Sensible? No?"

Mom sniffed. "When did you eat last?" she asked.

"I've been eating and eating." I brought the sack of hazelnuts out of my pocket. "Have some," I offered.

Mom protested that they were fattening, but we both had some. Before either of us had fattened perceptibly, however, all hell broke loose.

There was this sudden screaming, both human screaming and automotive. Every Greek in the shadow of the Acropolis seemed to be under our windows giving anguished voice. Every brake on every wheel in the Balkans seemed to be down there screaming. I dove for the balcony. As I got to the balustrade and leaned over, there rose toward me a hubbub of excited voices. The street was full of people, and the roadway was full of cars. All traffic had screeched to a dead stop. Some of the people down there were looking up at me and gesticulating wildly. Others were rushing toward a heap of something that lay in the street. I had only a moment before the crowd closed in so tight around it that they cut if off from my view, but it was long enough. It was the second time I'd had only a moment before losing sight of it, but it was brown and it had that purplish surface glow to it. I told myself sternly that thinking I smelled Lily of Luxor was pure imagination, not twelve stories above the street, not even with a strong updraft.

Mrs. Grymm, more tremulously fluty than ever, called to me. "Mr. Erridge. Are you on the balcony, Mr. Erridge?"

"Yes, Mrs. Grymm. It's all right. It's down in the street, some sort of accident."

"I know. Somebody jumped or fell. I can't come out. I've taken my girdle off, and I'm a sight. I saw it, Mr. Erridge. It came from above, hurtled right past my window and me with practically nothing on." She gave a little, hysterical laugh. "I did the silliest thing," she said. "I just pulled the drapes across my window, as though it mattered if someone who jumped or fell did see me, and anyhow whoever it was couldn't any more. It was way down below here by then."

Mom spoke from right beside me. "How horrible," she said. "Are you all right, my dear? Would you like me to come sit with you a while?"

"Oh, no, dear. I'm all right. I'm getting ready for bed."

"That's the right idea," I told her. Putting my arm around Mom, I took her back inside. "What about you getting ready for bed, too?"

She shuddered. "I'll have nightmares," she said.

I fixed her a drink. She didn't demur. I downed the one I'd left waiting around. Nobody was worrying about how it would go on top of the *ouzoo* and champagne.

"I wonder how your buddy, Grymm, looks with her girdle off," I said, not because I could possibly care but just in the hope of diverting Mom from one horror by setting her to imagining another.

It worked. It got her turned off to a minor worry.

"Matthew," she said, "I hope you aren't going to mind her being around. She is such a good soul, and nobody's ever been kinder to me. What with her Greek being so good and her knowing the country so well and her being such a solid, no-nonsense sort of person, I'm afraid I've been imposing on her."

"Oh, I don't mind," I assured her. "Just tell me how you ever got far enough past first impressions to find out about her kind heart."

Mom almost smiled. "I know what you mean," she said. "The first impression is dreadful. I was in the writing room at the Achilles. I was writing to you. I'd been reading your last letter. She was at the desk facing me. You know how they have them in those facing pairs. The first I was aware of her she was asking me if she could have the stamps. She sends them to some child back home for his collection."

Mom let her have the stamps. Then the next time they ran into each other, they chatted a bit.

"She's lonely, of course," Mom said. "Then yesterday when I just didn't know how I was ever going to get away from that policeman after he'd brought me back to the Achilles, I used her."

To hear Mom tell it, she'd been devious and calculating and all that jazz. Spotting Grymm across the lobby, she had told her boy with the busy hand that she had a friend she had to talk to and she had to catch her friend before friend would get away.

"She saved me, Matthew," Mom said. "That absurd man took one look at her, and he all but ran."

I've told you how Mom, while I was talking to her on the phone from the back gate to nowhere, suddenly relaxed when she thought of hiding out on that Athens-By-Night tour. That was the beginning of her plan. It grew from there. If she could manage to have Mrs. Grymm with her, she could cool her eager cop so easily. He wasn't going to want to take the two of them around the Athens tourists never see.

"I looked her up first thing this morning, and I told her about the idiotic man. She couldn't have been sweeter. All I have to do is mention anything and she gets the whole thing arranged before I could even begin to find out what to do. When I said, for instance, that if I knew of a good hotel, I'd move, she came right up with this lovely place and insisted on moving over here with me, which, of course, was an enormous comfort to me. And she's so kind that she won't even let you thank her. She keeps insisting that she's always preferred it over here. The only reason she went to the Achilles at all was because she was lonely, and it is the place where you find all the Americans."

It was easy to see what was bugging Mom. I had come, and she didn't need Grymm any more. She was going to feel like a heel sloughing her ogre off now that she had her knight in battered armor.

"And she is fun to be with," Mom went on, pushing it hard. "She has such good Greek, and she knows the country so well that it's almost like seeing it with a native."

"Furthermore," I said, "she doesn't pat you. As a matter of fact, this language thing has me licked. I can easily get to the place where I won't be able to do without her."

"You'll find yourself liking her more and more," Mom told me.

"I'll try not to overdo it," said I, giving it the lighter touch.

I was even merry about it, but that doesn't say Erridge was his usual carefree self. I kept waiting for the knock to come at my door, not the five-pause-three combo because I was convinced I'd taken care of that, but a visit from the fuzz. Hadn't brown suit, before he jumped or fell, clearly established himself at the Queen's Palace Hotel as a cat whose business would be with Erridge? Hadn't he displayed an eagerness to meet with Erridge that hadn't been matched by any eagerness on Erridge's part?

Ordinarily I don't go out looking for trouble. I can wait till it comes to me; but now we had those connecting rooms, and I didn't see how it could come to me without coming to Mom as well. I wasn't sure that even if I went out to meet it, I could keep it within comfortable bounds, namely away from Mom, but I could try.

I tossed the last of my whiskey into me and blew Mom a kiss. "I'm going downstairs to see what all the hoorah's about."

Mom looked bleak. "Mind if I don't go with you, Matthew?"

"No," I told her. "You go to bed."

I didn't have to wait for the elevator to come up. It was

parked there on the twelfth floor just the way we had left it. I punched the button for the lobby. When the car stopped, and the door slid open, I came face to face with the hall porter. For a man so recently tipped, he should have looked happier to see me.

He moved fast. "Get yourself out of sight," he whispered. "Your foreigner friend with the bandaged hand is dead out there in the street. Nobody knows him, and nobody's told the police you know him. Keep out of sight." I started to say something, but he wasn't listening. Planting the flat of his hand on my chest, he pushed me back into the car, and hit the button for basement.

"Right to the left of the elevator," he whispered. "Staff locker room. Wait in there for me."

I started on a word of protest, but he cut me off. "I'm not taking these risks for you," he snarled. "You get yourself mixed up with these people, you can take your chances. It's for your mama."

With that he stepped back and let the door shut. The car dropped to the basement. The hallway down there was lighted the way the bar was upstairs. To the left was a door with a faint glow of light coming through its glass panel. I opened it and went in. There were the usual benches a man can sit on when he's pulling his pants on or changing his shoes. Instead of lockers the place had parallel wooden partitions, each with a row of hooks on it. Street clothes hung there while the men were on duty, uniforms while they were off duty. All except one of the hooks on the partition that faced the door had stuff hanging on them, street clothes or uniforms. The one was bare except that it had a pair of shoes on the floor right below it. For want of anything better to do I sit on that first bench and light a cigarette.

My mind takes off on its own, wondering who goes on duty and changes nothing but his shoes. I'm being good, doing as I'm told. So what happens?

The lights go out. Even as the dark comes down on me, I know which lights they are. They're mine, and they've been turned off at the main switch, the place where head meets back of neck, just at the base of the skull. One sharp blow will do it. The lights go out.

VI

Surfacing under a wet towel, I looked up at the hall porter. He wasn't looking friendly.

"A fine time to go fainting away," he said.

I wasn't going to answer that until I was up off the flat of my back. He put out a hand to help me. I shook him off.

"Never mind," I said. "I do better without your help."

"That," he said, "is gratitude."

"Look, Charlie. I'm not forgetting who sent me down here."

"Maybe you can remember this then. It's no good talking tough with me. I know better. Nobody even lays a hand on you, and you faint dead away just from fright. If I let the police have you, you'd be so scared, you'd be dropping dead."

"So that's going to be the story," I growled.

He growled right back at me. "We've still got the police all over us, and we can't do anything until they're gone. But then we're going to throw your friend, Leonidas, out of the hotel."

He had his own plans for what he would contribute toward expediting Kostya's departure, but he explained that he was going to have to share the joy with every other able-bodied man on the hotel staff. When they were through with the Spartan, they were never going to be seeing him around the premises again.

"You," he continued, "are lucky you have your mama. If you were here alone, we'd do you along with Leonidas."

He repeated his run through of the detailed violences of the throwing-out process, but now wistfully. It was all the fun they could have taking Erridge apart and tossing him piece by piece out into the gutter. It was the fun they were passing up out of consideration for Mom.

"Me ducking the police was your idea," I said, "not mine. You know what I think?"

"Nobody cares what you think. You're getting off easy. So you'll do as you're told."

"So the police won't know the kind of hotel you're running?"

He conceded that much. The hotel's good name was part of it. They were saving what they could. A man jumping or falling from one of their balconies wasn't going to bring tourists.

"Two men fight over a pretty boy," he added. "One of the men gets murdered. We want that kind of a name for the hotel?"

There were too many pieces of that, and they all needed denying. "The man was pushed?" I asked.

"You telling me or asking me?"

"Jumped, fell, or pushed," I said. "He started above the twelfth floor. Mrs. Grymm saw him come tumbling by. I didn't even see him. I was in my room with my mother."

"Your mama," he sighed. "Your mama's friend. Who'll believe them?"

He ran it down for me. The police had a murder they didn't know a thing about, not even that it was a murder. Why were they so ignorant? Because there wasn't anybody, whether man or woman, in that hotel who wasn't head over heels in love with Erridge's mama. The hotel people knew everything, and they were telling the police nothing. All Erridge had to do was behave himself, and it would stay that way. He was going to get away with murder.

What did they know? He told me:

Item 1: Erridge checked into the hotel in a state of dishevelment. Anybody could see he'd been in a fight.

Item 2: Erridge, in the face of all accepted custom, let no one carry his bag for him. Nobody could touch it.

Item 3: The chambermaid, turning Erridge's bed down for

the night, examined the precious bag and found a bloodstain on the leather. The chambermaid was a Cypriote. She knew blood when she saw it.

Item 4: The murdered man came to the hotel to find Erridge.

Item 5: Erridge showed unwillingness to be found by the murdered man. Erridge was interested only in Constantine Leonidas, and all Athens knew what Leonidas was.

Item 6: The murdered man had a recent knife cut on his hand. Comparisons could be made between the stain on Erridge's bag and the blood of the dead man.

Item 7: Immediately after the murder, Erridge came down to the lobby in panic flight. Avoiding the police in the lobby, he went on to the basement where his control broke, and he fainted.

While he was talking, I saw something. I interrupted.

"When you came down here and found me," I asked, "was there anyone in here but me?"

"Nobody," he said, making no secret of his strained patience. "That's why I told you to come here. There's nobody here ever except when we're going on or off shift."

"Nobody came in while you were bringing me around?"

"Nobody. I have the door locked."

"I've got news for you. I didn't faint. The shoes are gone. Somebody was here. He came up behind me. He was an expert. He knew just where to chop me. He went off with the shoes."

"Who's going to believe that? You have your shoes on."

Even while he was telling me off, however, his gaze was straying down the line of hooks. He broke off and with a pointing finger he began counting hooks. He came to the empty one, the one where I'd seen just the pair of shoes. Now it was completely empty, no shoes.

He blinked and looked again. He rubbed his eyes and took another look. He began muttering in Greek. He walked down there and examined the space closely. He dropped to his knees and searched under the bench.

"I saw the shoes there before I got knocked cold," I said. "They're not there now."

He came back into English. "The shoes," he growled. "The pants, the shirt, the coat, all my street clothes."

"There's never anyone in here this time of night," I said. "Tonight was different. There was somebody here stealing your clothes. He heard me coming and ducked back of the partition, out of sight. He didn't have time to scoop up all your stuff before I came in here. He had to leave the shoes, but that was all right. He snuck around the partition, came up behind me, and blipped me. Then he lifted your shoes along with the rest of your stuff. He took off before you got down."

The man was on the verge of tears. He called attention to the clothes still hanging on the other hooks, to all the other shoes ranged along the bench. He said his stuff hadn't been the worst of the lot, but he pointed out shirts and coats and pants and shoes which he insisted were newer and in far better shape than his had been.

"A thief," he moaned. "He can take Alexander's new jacket, Agamemnon's new pants—he bought them only yesterday and wore them the first time today. He can take George's new shoes. He leaves all this and steals only what is mine. Why?"

"Size," I suggested. "Your stuff fits him."

"He steals my clothes to wear them?"

"What else? If he's stealing stuff to sell it, he takes what will bring the best price. If he's stealing clothes to wear, he has to take what will fit him best."

He sighed and looked at his watch. "I've been away from the lobby too long," he said. "I'll take you back to your room. Then I must be at my desk."

"You telling the police about your stuff being stolen?" I asked.

He laughed bitterly. "I'm telling them," he said. "It'll do me no good. You never get anything back, but I'm telling them. It will explain my being down here so long."

I offered to go with him and be a witness for him. He would have none of that, even though he was now thinking a bit better of Erridge. He no longer had the idea that I had just fainted away. He was striking from the record one of the charges he had brought against me; but it was, after all, the least of the charges, and I should, therefore, not have expected it to make too great a difference in his attitude. Actually it seemed to be making a disproportionate difference. The way I dug it, the other charges still stood, but the man's confidence in them had been shaken a little.

He came around to reasoning with me. He didn't need a witness. He'd done nothing except having his clothes swiped, unless you wanted to say he'd been withholding information from the police, and it would do him no good to tell them that. He could explain his having gone down to the basement. He could say he had come down to sneak a smoke, but what could I say? How would Erridge explain going down to the staff locker room? Erridge could smoke anywhere he liked.

I argued with him. Somehow I'd become involved with these men, Leonidas and the dead man. The dead man I'd seen only once, briefly in Cairo, and then only a back view of him when he was stealing my bag. Unaccountably he had returned my bag, and nothing was missing from it. Leonidas I had first seen at the air terminal, and he had ever since been trying to attach himself to me. It was all very well to assume he'd been making the try for the obvious reasons anyone would attribute to Leonidas, but now that he seemed to be connected with the dead man, there would have to be some other reason.

"You don't like what's been happening," I said. "I like it even less. I want the police to hear my whole story."

I was crazy. The dead man was dead. He wouldn't be bothering me any more. Leonidas would be thrown out of the hotel. He gave me his solemn assurance that, when he and his colleagues finished with the Spartan, Leonidas would know better than to bother me or any other Queen's Palace Hotel guest ever again. The whole business would finish right here.

"You talk to the police," he said, "and you will do nothing but make trouble. You will make trouble for me, for the manager, for the chambermaid, for all of us here in the hotel. We will have all the questions to answer. Why didn't we tell the police this? Why didn't we tell them that? We will be ruined, all of us. And that's only the beginning of the trouble. It will be trouble for you."

"Not for me. The police can check with Cairo. The American Embassy knows what happened there, and the Cairo police know."

"I know the police here, and you don't," he insisted. "It will be trouble for you and for your lady mama. It will be much trouble for your lady mama and for her friend, Mrs. Grymm. Mrs. Grymm, you say, saw the man fall past the twelfth floor. The police will ask why she's been saying nothing."

"She was getting ready for bed. She had her corset off."

"She has the telephone in her room. You can call down to the desk without a corset. We have been taking risks for you, terrible risks for you and your mama, and her friend, Mrs. Grymm. You can't do this to us."

"Nobody asked you to stick your neck out for us."

"Your lady mama. She asked us."

"She asked you what?"

"She asked us to make you comfortable, to give you anything you needed, to see you would be all right till she got back to the hotel."

I shook my head. "You think she meant hiding me from the police?"

"Anything you needed, Mr. Erridge."

We were getting nowhere except that maybe I was coming to see the whole thing in full perspective. I was of two minds about the hotel people. It was just possible that they were in on this caper, whatever the caper was. I hadn't forgotten the way I'd been delivered to the Queen's Palace Hotel. There was a mystery there that needed clearing up, but there was also the fact that Mom was at the hotel, and her story of how she came there wouldn't mesh with any of my suspicions. I had to believe the hotel people were clean. Of course, they had been making every possible kind of mistake sticking their necks out for me; but they had been doing it for me. I wasn't quite ready to chop them off. I tried to make a deal instead.

"What's your name?" I asked the hall porter.

"Paul."

"Okay, Paul. I'll let you take me back to my room. I'll say nothing to the police, but on one condition."

His head reached up in that Greek nod that means no.

"When the police leave," I said past his refusal, "and you go to work on Leonidas, I want to be there. I want you to come by my room. I'll leave the door open. You won't have to knock or wake the ladies, but you come for me before you go get Leonidas. I want first crack at him. He's got to tell me what's been happening to me."

I don't know what condition he'd been expecting me to make. This one was all right. We even shook on it.

Upstairs I found Mom in bed, sound asleep. I wanted to be grateful for it, but it wasn't easy to dig. She'd never been that cold blooded, but there she was sleeping like a baby. Just before I switched her lights off for her, I found the explanation, a vial of sleeping pills on the dressing table. Mom had taken one or two of those and knocked herself out.

Pulling out to my room, I shut the connecting door on my side, fixed myself a drink, and took it out to the balcony. Down in the street everything seemed to be back to normal. The body had been removed, and traffic had again come to full boil. I set my drink down on the parapet while I lighted a cigarette. I was only on my first drag of smoke when the phone rang inside.

I dove for it. I didn't think it could wake Mom, but it was no good taking any chances. I snatched it off the cradle, and all I got was that sound. You know it, the practical joker's click. Some cat calls you. You pick it up, and right off he's not there. I dial the desk. The operator says the desk didn't call, and the hall porter didn't call.

I'm still on the phone when Paul shows at my door. I start giving him some hell. He denies ringing me. Any guest in any room can dial any other room direct.

"Leonidas," Paul says. "He calls you. Before you answer, he hears us outside his door. He hangs up."

"He hears you outside his door? We made a deal. I get first crack at him."

"Nobody's going in till we get up there," Paul said.

It's an army up on the fourteenth floor. The manager, a couple of assistant managers, a covey of tough-looking porters, a platoon of muscular bellhops. Every last man of them had a leather belt wrapped around his hand with the buckle end swinging loose. They're all set to hash him up and stuff him into vine leaves.

Paul whips his own belt off and wraps it around his hand. They're all looking at me, but I give them the upward nod. I'm going in there unarmed. I'm not even wearing my worry beads. Paul brings out the passkey. Nobody bothers to knock or anything like that, and nobody is bothering to stand back in case the Spartan should come out shooting.

Paul hauls the door open and hits the light switch. The posse is lining up according to rank, but I don't wait for anybody to tell me where I fit in. I shoulder past the manager, and I go through the door at Paul's heels. The room is empty. There's no one in the bathroom, and no one in the closet. There's nobody out on the balcony.

The closet door stands open. All the bureau drawers have been pulled out. The wastepaper basket has been tipped over and is lying on its side. The bed has been pulled apart.

So there's nobody there but us Avengers, but nobody's unwinding any belt from his hand. Nobody's relaxing. The boys are gathering in a tight circle around Erridge. They're licking their lips. They're looking hungry.

"You're hiding him in your room," the manager says, speaking for them. "It won't work. He can't get out of the hotel."

"Why can't he?"

"He can't get through the lobby."

I don't ask what's to stop him while every able-bodied man in the place is up on the fourteenth floor. I'm moving slowly, and they're moving with me. They don't seem to mind as long as I'm not heading for the balcony or the door out to the hall. They're holding me in that room. What they plan to do to me seems to be waiting on developments. Experimentally I back off from the manager. He follows after me with his men at his shoulder. They're not closing the distance on me, just moving as I move, keeping it constant. I have nothing to go on but the feel of the thing, but I'm remembering the way they automatically fell into line strictly according to rank. I tell myself that nothing's going to happen until the manager starts it.

I concentrate on the manager. I haven't forgotten that I have some of his troops behind me. I'm going to like it better when I have all of them where I can see them. There's that place at the back of my head, down there at the base of my skull just above where my neck joins on. Those cats behind me can be holding their ground, and then it'll be that I'm beginning to crowd them. I want to glance back over my shoulder and check up on them, but I'm not taking my eyes off the manager. If and when he gives the signal, I have to be ready to move.

As I think about that place at the back of my head, I have to fight off a yen to put my hand up there and touch it. I can't spare the hands. Any moment now I'm going to need them, both of them. But I have this crazy idea that the place back there is feeling mushy. If the babies I'm backing into let their belt buckles swing, I know where they'll be aiming them.

After all, I'd had it right on that spot down in the basement locker room. I keep my eyes fixed on the manager. He's throwing no signals. Then I see them edging around in the corners of my vision, and I know I'm not crowding those buckos who'd been circled in behind me. They're oozing out to either side. One more step, or at most two, and I'll be feeling the wall against my shoulder blades. I'm going to feel a lot better when I have the old patting area flat against the wall, and it will be only a semicircle of the Queen's Palace guard hemming me in. Not that it's the patting area I'm worrying about. It's that place where the Erridge head meets the Erridge neck.

I watch the manager, but I talk to the hall porter. "Paul," I say. "When you go off duty, you go down to the basement and change. Do you show yourself in the lobby in the clothes you wear to and from work or do you go out by a basement entrance?"

The manager gives no signal, but Paul steps out of rank. Since he has to get past the two assistant managers and the manager to come at me, I have time to set myself. He has the buckle swinging, and he's swinging it high. I know what he's after, and it's something I'm not going to let him have. I don't have any eyes I'm ready to spare.

I'm ducking in under it, planning to take him in the gut, but I get an unexpected break. The manager grabs at him as he comes by. It isn't enough to stop him, but it does swing him a bit off balance. Swinging with it, I get my left shoulder into him while I'm reaching up with my right hand and catching the belt between his hand and the swinging buckle.

The way they teach it, you grab him around the wrist. A quick tug at his arm just as your shoulder slams into him, and that does it. He goes flying across your back, and halfway across the room he hits the floor hard. The belt makes it even better. It's as though he has an arm that is six inches longer than normal. The way he's anchored the belt by wrapping it around his hand, it's perfectly secure. The harder you pull on it, the tighter it goes around his hand, the less chance there is it'll slip.

If you dig leverage at all, Charlie, you know that the longer your lever, the bigger your result and the smaller your effort. Get the timing right on it, and it's never hard to do, but with that extra advantage it's as easy as tiddlying a tiddlywink. My one problem is it's likely to be too good. He'll hit the floor so hard that he won't even be in shape for talking to, and I don't know that there's anybody else in that room I can talk to.

But Erridge is running in luck. Paul does come down hard, but there's all that bedding and those blankets that have been pulled off the bed and left heaped on the floor. He lands in the middle of that, and it's like a stack of wrestling mats. He doesn't even have the wind knocked out of him. All he needs is a moment, and that's for nothing but getting past his surprise, to come back to where he digs which end is up.

The manager uses that moment to bark out an order. The troops all drop back a pace; and Paul, who's ready to come charging back up at me, changes his mind and stays where he is, doing nothing but looking baleful.

"He's your size, Paul," I say, going right on with my argument. "Use your head, man. Mrs. Grymm is in the room right under here. She saw the body hurtle past. From where? From here, of course. How did the room get the way it is? Who was looking for what? Not Leonidas. He wasn't searching his own room, was he? It was the man in the brown suit. He was looking for something. That's how the blood got on my bag. It was from his hand. He was looking there, and he was looking up here. They fought. Leonidas pushed him off the balcony."

"You helped him get away. You helped him steal my clothes."

The manager's stern eye on him kept Paul where he was. It didn't keep him from snarling at me.

"Did I go down to the locker room on my own?" I ask. "Who sent me down there? You did. Leonidas has shoved brown suit off the balcony. What does he do then? He gets himself out of the hotel and clean away from here as fast as he can. He can't go out by the lobby, and he doesn't want to go out looking any more like himself than he can help. He rides the elevator down to the basement. He hits the locker room. He finds himself some threads that'll fit, and it's your bad luck you're his size. He's in the locker room changing when I come in. So I'm between him and the door. He has to get past me to get out. He comes up behind me and blips me on the back of the head. I don't hear him because he has his shoes off. That does it for him. All he has to do then is step into your shoes and take off."

"Where are his clothes then?" Paul isn't snarling any more. He's just asking.

"He took them with him, bundled them up and carried them out with him. What would you expect him to do?"

The manager unwound the belt from around his hand. Most

of the rest of them did the same without waiting for orders. Some of the boys in the lower echelons—a couple of the porters and a few bellhops—seemed reluctant, but the manager snapped out a command. Obviously it was the Greek for "dismissed." The troops filed out, and now they were all threading their belts through the loops on their pants as they went. I was left with Paul and the manager.

"Ever since I got here," I said, "I've been listening to you. Now you're going to listen to me."

Starting with my landing in Cairo, I gave them the whole story. If it mystified them, I wasn't digging any of it either, but I knew what I was doing next. I was going to have the fuzz back. I knew it was way past midnight, but I was going to start with the American Embassy. There had to be someone over there to handle emergencies on a twenty-four-hour basis, and Erridge was having an emergency that wasn't going to wait till morning. I was getting me an embassy man so that, when there would be some interpreting to do, I'd know I wasn't being snowed.

I hurt their feelings. They both brought out their beads and clicked away, soothing their nerves. What I proposed would get them in trouble with the authorities. It would be the ruin of the hotel. It was always better to stay uninvolved.

"If what I've been is uninvolved," I told them, "I'm trying involvement."

We kicked it around and worked out a bit of a compromise. I started out plumping for the truth, the whole T, and nothing but the T. They started out wanting to leave things lay. Where we came out I figured to gain more than I was conceding. We were going to fudge it just enough to cover for them. I would say nothing about going down to the locker room. I could tell the fuzz the rest of it, if I would do my hotel friends the favor of leaving that one bit out.

The story would be that Erridge had been completely unaware that the dead man was brown suit. Paul would say that when, on viewing the body, he said he didn't know the man, he had just forgotten. Thinking about it later, it had come to seem to him that there was something familiar about brown suit, and finally it had come to him. The man had been in earlier in the evening asking for Mr. Erridge. As soon as Paul had remembered, he'd gone up to Mr. Erridge's room to ask him about brown suit, at which point Mr. Erridge had told Paul this shocking story of the harrassment of a foreign visitor, and everyone had agreed that the fuzz must know.

"How do we tell them about Leonidas then?" I asked.

The manager had that part of it. He'd been doing a tour of the building, something he did at fairly frequent intervals. He found the door of Leonidas's room open and the room in its present state of disorder. Mr. Erridge's description of one of the men who'd been harrassing him fitted Constantine Leonidas perfectly. Both the hotel people and Mr. Erridge felt that the police had to know.

"You're going to have to sell this story to an awful lot of people," I reminded them. "You had your whole army up here."

That they shrugged off. The men would say exactly what they were told to say. They were all Greeks, and the less a Greek has to mess with the fuzz, the better he likes it. Crazy about it I wasn't, but they did make it begin to sound reasonable, and I was beginning to take a liking to these cats. They had a good kind of toughness, and they worked hard to make the drachma.

They'd jumped to insulting conclusions about Erridge. From where they'd been sitting who was this Erridge? He was mama's boy, and if you don't know the kind of trouble mama's boy tourists go looking for when they're loose on the shores of the Mediterranean, you just haven't traveled.

"Let's lead it into the wooden horse," I said, "and see if it takes Troy."

I went back to my room. Paul and the manager went down to the lobby. Paul rang through to the embassy for me. The drink I'd left out on the terrace parapet I brought in so I could work on it while I was hanging on the phone. I listened to a lot of Greek. Then a voice came on, and it talked American, State Department brand.

I took it over. "A man," I explained, "jumped, fell, or was pushed off one of the balconies here at the Queen's Palace Hotel tonight. Now I learn that he came to the hotel asking for me. I don't know what's going on or how I'm mixed up in it; but it's going on, and I am mixed up in it. I want to tell the police my story. I don't think it can be left for morning; and if there's any language problem, I'd like an embassy man on hand to do the interpreting."

"But Mr. Erridge. How can you be involved?"

"Just what we've got to find out. It's only a matter of time before the police will be here to pick me up for murder."

There was a gasp at the other end. "Pick you up? What is this?"

"It started in Cairo yesterday. I had magnificent cooperation from our embassy there."

I dropped a couple of the Cairo names, and embassy night watch told me to sit tight. Somebody would be right over.

"Have somebody bring the fuzz with him," I suggested.

"You don't want to tell us your story before you take it to the police?"

"No," I said. "It's past my bedtime already."

"Have you been drinking, Mr. Erridge?"

"Moderately. I'm not drunk. Shall I walk the straight telephone line over to your office?"

"No, Mr. Erridge. Sit tight, Mr. Erridge. I'll have a man over there right away, Mr. Erridge. He'll have the police with him, Mr. Erridge."

So I lay on my bed, and I finished my drink, and I studied that picture of the titmouse. Along with her other peculiarities, she had taken to slipping in and out of focus. I didn't go for that. It was unsettling. Just watching her do it was making my gut turn over. It was only when I closed my eyes and kept them closed that my gut came upright again. That was it. Just letting my eyes close took care of me fine.

When I opened them again, the gut was back where it belonged. There was something wrong with my head. It felt as though somebody had packed it in excelsior and was ready to ship it off somewhere by air freight. There was a powerful smell of coffee coming at my nostrils, and even just the smell of it was beginning to unpack my head.

I wasn't going to let that bug me. There were too many other things. There was the view from the window, which was the Parthenon with the sun standing high over it. There was Mom hanging over me with the cup of coffee. She was all dressed for the day, and she was trying to fit her face to a look that was neither worried nor disapproving. There was Matthew Erridge neatly tucked in under the bedsheets with all his clothes off.

VII

It was getting on toward noon. Mom was tactfully saying
nothing about drinking more than I could handle. Have you ever
been around a woman who is resolutely refraining from speaking
her mind? The silence gets to be deafening. None of the hotel
people I knew were available. My buddies on the night staff
wouldn't be coming on again until later in the afternoon.

The next couple of hours were a drag. I shooed Mom out of
the room while I shaved, showered, and dressed. I suggested that
she pick up her buddy, Mrs. Grymm, for lunch and sight-seeing,
shopping, or what-have-you. Matthew had some business with
the embassy, and he didn't know how long it was going to keep
him.

For finding the embassy, I didn't have to put any trust in
any cab driver. We picked up Mom's hired heap. I drove it.
Grymm handled the navigation. I dropped them at the place
they'd picked for lunch, but Grymm plotted a route that took
us past the embassy. All I had to do was retrace a little. For that
kind of navigation I could easily learn to live with the way
Grymm looked and sounded.

The embassy knew all about Matthew Erridge. They'd already had a bellyful of Matthew Erridge. The embassy was
always at the service of the traveling American, but the traveling
American had to recognize that the service didn't include running around to the traveling American's hotel just to undress the
traveling American and tuck him under the sheets. Even when

the embassy wasn't tied up with such stuff as the Greco-Turkish rumble in Cyprus, the traveling American could undress himself and put himself to bed, or he could sleep where he fell and with his clothes on.

The glass that had held the last drink I remembered taking had been sitting on the bedside table when I woke. I'd wrapped that glass carefully in a lot of tissues, and I had it with me. I brought it out, unwrapped it, and set it on the embassy cat's desk. Giving it a look Carry Nation would have envied, he begged me to put it away.

"Mr. Erridge," he said, every word having been wrung out in outrage, "you're not going to start drinking again, not here, not now?"

"I was slipped a mickey," I said.

"Now, really, Mr. Erridge. Must you be so lurid?"

I explained that the glass was not for drinking, not even for touching. It was for analysis. I wanted that glass put in the hands of a good, reliable lab. There could be just enough residue dried on to the goblet. I didn't much care whether the additive I'd taken with my whiskey was some kind of sleeping medicine or something local like worry-bead juice. I wanted it firmly in the record that Erridge had been drugged.

"Drugged once," I said, "slugged twice, and bugged all over."

Before he'd listen to my story, I had to hear his. He had a dossier on Citizen Erridge, and, point by point, it built for any impartial observer a clear, curt, complete picture of Citizen Erridge.

The man was a hallucinated lush. He was a pain in the calipygian parts. He had been making a career of bugging embassy staffs and the police on two continents. He'd turned up in Cairo with a skinful and promptly lost his bag at the airport. The first the embassy there heard of him, he was calling out of hours to report that he had on arrival in his Cairo hotel room lost everything else he owned right down to his worthless pelt. His complaint of persecution by an unknown who reeked of Lily of Luxor hair oil, considered in retrospect, was patently incredible.

It was now Cairo's considered opinion that there had been a simple mixup in luggage at the airport, that later at the hotel Erridge in drunken confusion had given the clothes off his back to the hotel valet for valeting and had neglected to remove therefrom his passport, money, and other such valuables. It was much to the credit of the Egyptians that, even as a result of so gross an indiscretion, Erridge suffered no loss. He recovered everything.

So much for Cairo. In Athens this same Erridge telephoned the embassy at a most shocking hour, crying murder. He insisted that an embassy man call on him at his hotel immediately, bringing the police with him. When diplomat and fuzz hastened to the hotel and went to Erridge's room, they found this most troublesome cat stretched out on his bed with all his clothes on. He hadn't undressed. He hadn't turned off the lights. He hadn't crawled between the sheets. Nothing could have been more obvious than Erridge's drunken stupor. The hotel staff, renowned throughout the Hellenic world for honesty, reliability, and courtesy, had been naturally reluctant to discuss the drinking habits of a patron, but they had been forced to admit that Mr. Erridge had arrived at the hotel already in a state of confused befuddlement. To their own knowledge, he had taken no intermission in his drinking, imbibing not only much, but in most unwise combinations. The greater part of a bottle of champagne in the hotel bar, some quantity of *ouzoo* at the cafe across the avenue, and a considerable dosage of one-hundred-proof whiskey up in his room.

As the police knew, there had been a most unfortunate accident at the hotel that evening. By an odd coincidence the victim of the accident had been most noticeably redolent of a hair oil so popular with Egyptians that there was probably not a hotel man in all of the Mediterranean area who could not at first sniff spot the provenance of an Egyptian guest.

Since Mr. Erridge had come to Athens by way of Cairo, he evidently had considerable familiarity with this most noticeable scent. On nothing more than this tenuous evidence of his nostrils, Erridge, it appeared, had come down with the notion that the unfortunate victim of that unfortunate accident had come to his death through following Erridge across the sea from Cairo.

The concluding remarks put the lid on it. Once the embassy man I'd brought out in the wee hours was there anyhow, he had done what he could for me. He'd fed the police the boys-will-be-boys bit, soothed them down, and with the thanks of the embassy sent them back to their interrupted card game at headquarters. He had stood by as an observer while Paul, assisted by a platoon of bellhops, saw to my comfort. They had undressed me. They had tucked me in. They had turned out the lights. They had tiptoed away.

"We hope, Mr. Erridge," this embassy baby finished, "that you will tip them accordingly. They gave you far more service and far more consideration than the contract calls for. We cannot hope that mere money will redeem our image in their eyes; but really, sir, generous tips all around. It is the least you can do."

"Before they're tucked into the pokey," I said.

"Mr. Erridge, could you be persuaded to leave the country?"

"I just came. I haven't even talked to the police yet."

He sighed, but he listened. I handed him the whole history. I took it all the way back to first touching down in Cairo, and I left nothing out. He listened, but there was only one thing wrong. As I told it, I was having trouble believing it myself. I even caught myself apologizing for it.

"I know this sounds impossible," I said, "but the police can check it out. I have the shield number of the cop who drove the cab to the Queen's Palace Hotel. I have the cab medallion number. I have the nut peddler's note."

He read the note carefully. He studied it. He was giving it proper consideration, but he was also giving himself time to recover from shock. When he finally spoke, he was at his most tight-lipped and censorious.

"Even without your story, Mr. Erridge," he said, "this is obviously a note written by a male prostitute to arrange an assignation in the face of the violent opposition of his protector. You want to show this to the police, and you want to tell them that you responded to it with a suggestion that you would go to his room instead of his coming to yours. Really, Mr. Erridge, what construction can you possibly expect them to put on that?"

"You're oversimplifying," I protested. As far as I could remember the exact wording, I quoted to him the contents of the note I slipped under Leonidas's door, threats and all.

"Seriously, Mr. Erridge, you don't think these suggestions of sadism will improve your position?"

"Knowing what goes on might improve my position. Putting the police hep to what goes on should improve it. All I'm asking of the embassy is that you provide me with a reliable interpreter."

"And a chemical analysis of that empty glass."

"Just steer me to a reliable lab."

"We'll take care of it for you, Mr. Erridge."

"I'll pay for the analysis," I said, "and I want three certified copies of the report, one for you, one for the police, and one for me."

"If you like, but don't expect it to prove anything. Even if there should be traces of drugs, we'll still not know whether the drugs were present in the glass before you drank from it or after."

"I don't spit sleeping pills," I growled.

He shrugged. "You've put yourself in an embarrassing position with the police, Mr. Erridge."

"And I'm manufacturing evidence to improve my image?"

He was too much the diplomat to come out and tell me it was going to be what he would think. He put it all in terms of what the Greek authorities would think.

"All right," I told him. "Even if I'm getting it only for Erridge's satisfaction, I still want it."

After this embassy interview, the session with the fuzz was pure pleasure. I hardly needed my interpreter. He did pilot me to headquarters, and he had the right words to say to the right underlings. When the time came for Erridge to speak his piece, he had me settled in with a little committee of upper-echelon police officers all of whom were beautifully English speaking. They were also beautifully polite. Any time anything was said in Greek, they quickly translated it for me. All the embassy man had to do was provide verification. He was insurance.

I gave them the whole wild history, again beginning with my arrival in Cairo. Whatever they thought of it, they took it dead pan. They asked no question and made no comments. They interrupted me only once and then only to act on information I gave them. It was when I came to my arrival at the Queen's Palace Hotel. They congratulated me on having thought of taking the numbers of the cop and the cabbie. There was a time out, but only to issue an order for the cop to report in and an order for the hackie to be picked up for questioning.

When I had told it all, they took me to the Axilles. They waited out front while I went in with the interpreter. I handled it exactly as they told me to. We ambled up to the desk. It was a day clerk on duty. I introduced myself and asked if they had a message for me.

They had. Mrs. Erridge had left me a note, and the note was handed over. It said just what Mom told me she had written.

"I hope you haven't been inconvenienced, Mr. Erridge," the clerk said. "It's all my fault your not getting the note when you called around for it yesterday. I don't know how to apologize."

"Don't apologize," I said. "Just explain."

He explained. Mom handed the note in to him, and how he did such a thing he'll never know, but he absentmindedly slipped it into the wrong box. When he came on duty, the night man told him that a man, who said he was Mrs. Erridge's son, had demanded a message that wasn't there.

"I was appalled, Mr. Erridge. I thought he was crazy, Mr. Erridge. Then I went to this box for something else, and there it was looking right up at me, and I knew what I'd done. I don't know what to say, Mr. Erridge."

I reported back to the fuzz out front.

"Nice having that much of it cleared up," they said.

"Unless he's lying."

"Why would he lie, Mr. Erridge? His story does him no credit."

"Another story maybe does him even less credit," I said. "We need a story to explain my getting to the Queen's Palace Hotel." They were working on it. As soon as they picked the cabbie up and brought him in, we'd be getting to the bottom of that part of it.

Our next stop was the Queen's Palace. All through the ride over my fuzzy friends were deploring that clerk back at the Axilles. The way they dug it, a cat did much better at an old-fashioned Greek hotel like the Queen's Palace where things were done in the old-fashioned Greek way. The Greeks have a talent for the personal touch. They are incapable of learning the ways of the impersonally efficient machine. It happened all the time. As soon as a Greek tried to fit himself in as one of the cogs in a smoothly running mechanism, notes got into the wrong boxes. It could never have happened at the Queen's Palace. There every member of the staff would have been personally interested and personally concerned. Mom's note would have been passed lovingly from hand to hand, and it would have been the individual worry of every last man in the place to see that I got it.

The afternoon had been wearing along. The night staff had come on at the Queen's Palace. Paul was at his desk just inside the lobby door. The manager was hovering. The assistant managers were behind the registration desk. Scattered about the lobby were the muscular bellhops who'd been in our posse.

Picking up Paul and the manager, we set up shop in the manager's office. When informed that Mr. Erridge had accused them of withholding information from the police and was waiting only for a laboratory analysis of residues in his drinking glass before he charged them with using drugs on him, they looked only hurt and long-suffering.

The manager carried the ball. Paul opened up only when directly questioned. What Mr. Erridge was calling information withheld from the fuzz was either material so wildly irrelevant that they were confident the police wouldn't thank them for wasting police time with it or fancies so wildly Dionysiac that no sober man could credit them for a moment.

Now partly out of tact, since one of their own was involved, and partly out of a feeling that it would be wildly irrelevant, I hadn't bothered these police officers with any account of Mom's reasons for the move out of the Axilles. The manager brought that bit up.

For openers he said they would never have given Mr. Erridge a room if it hadn't been that his lady mama was already checked in and they were so charmed with her that they wanted to show her every consideration. She was a lady of the most delicate sensibilities and the strictest propriety. The gentlemen must understand how she came to the Queen's Palace in the first place. She had been driven out of the Axilles, and by what? Poor service? Chefs who didn't know *moussaka* from hamburger? No. The lady had taken flight from the friendly attentions of a police officer. You might call it narrow minded for a lady to take so much affront and affright from nothing more than a few kindly pats, but American ladies are used to different customs.

Many American ladies take to Greek customs with a delight that might even seem unseemly, but some do not; and it was important that such ladies be protected from shock. So there they are, chin-deep in the job of protecting Mom from the ruder realities when they have delivered to their doorstep a rude reality who is the poor, delicate lady's eagerly expected son.

Erridge arrives looking disreputable. His clothes are in a state. He is belligerent. They rush him through the lobby in the hope that no other guests will notice him, and they are praying he will have himself pulled together by the time his mama comes home.

It is quite true that he's saying he doesn't want the hotel. He wants a police station. It's apparent that in his confused state, he has some odd foreign notion that the honor of his mama has been smirched and that he must, by doing violence, expunge the stain.

"Gentlemen," the manager said, reaching an oratorical pitch that would have made Demosthenes spit out his pebbles and take a back seat in the *agora*, "can we permit a guest to go to the police station in that condition when it is so evident that he has nothing on his mind except committing assault on the person of a police officer?"

They do their best with Erridge, but shock follows shock. There's a bottle of whiskey in the gentleman's room. It was ordered for him by his mama, and they are thinking maybe they should have let the superb service slip just this once. This bugs them so much, it's a good thing they have their worry beads.

Then things begin to look better. Erridge returns to the lobby. He's cleaned himself up, and he's changed his clothes. He seems much calmer. The place gets so much ventilation from the sighs of relief that they turn off the air conditioning, but unfortunately he goes to some cafe where he drinks *ouzo*. Paul attests to the *ouzo*. The anise smell was unmistakable on Mr. Erridge's breath.

That, however, is the least of Paul's worries. The clerk on duty made the mistake of checking in a most unsavory character, one Constantine Leonidas, Spartan, undoubtedly known to the police. The management was not happy about having this Leonidas in the hotel, but he had checked in, and they could only hope that during his stay he might be on uncharacteristically good behavior and cause no scandal.

Also while Mr. Erridge is out, a man stops by to ask for him. This is a fat man in a brown suit, and he has on his head a perfumed hair oil much favored by Egyptians. When Paul tells Mr. Erridge that he's had a caller, Erridge's response horrifies Paul. Erridge makes it all too evident that he's been expecting a caller, but it is unmistakably the unsavory Leonidas.

Paul puts it to the fuzz as man to man. A lady is so puritanically American that she flees her hotel, horror-stricken by the kindly and harmless gallantry of a police officer. How can you let such a lady know that she has a son who will take up with the likes of Leonidas? Obviously you can't.

Paul pauses, and the manager takes over. He tells about the champagne, the ladies drinking only a little of it and Erridge consuming most of the bottle. He sees Erridge go upstairs with his mama, and he hopes that will settle this difficult man for the night. He confesses that shortly thereafter the problem of the indiscreet and alcoholic Mr. Erridge leaves his mind completely. There's the catastrophe of the gentleman who jumped or fell.

Finally, however, the body has been removed, and the manager has time to consider the matter of Constantine Leonidas. He explains that he has come to feel that one catastrophe in a single night was more than a respectable hotel could want on its premises; and this Leonidas, is he not a catastrophe? He goes up to Leonidas's room to evict the man, only to find that Leonidas, after the manner of his kind, has evidently decided that a hotel which for any reason at all has had police attention is no place for him. He has left. His room is vacant.

Unfortunately, while the manager is checking the room, Mr. Erridge turns up. He's evidently been putting whiskey on top of the *ouzoo*, the champagne and whatever he'd consumed before his arrival. He is disturbed by Leonidas's absence. Also he has heard that the man who jumped or fell was fat, dressed in a brown suit, and redolent of Egyptian hair oil. He's developed the delusion that the dead man and the man who'd been around asking for him are one and the same. He's full of some drunken fancy involving Leonidas and the dead man.

"We do our best to calm him and set him straight," the manager says, "but you know how it is with the fixed ideas of a drunk."

Erridge all this time is just listening. He's letting them lie all they like, but this gets to be too much. I turn to Paul. "You," I say, "told me they were the same man. Were you lying then, or are you lying now?"

Paul shrugs. He jerks his eyebrows up, and they carry his head with them. The manager welcomes my interruption. The gentlemen officers can see for themselves how delusional Mr. Erridge was under the influence of all that ill-assorted drink he had taken.

The fuzz knows the rest. The hotel people try to get Erridge to bed. They beg him not to call the embassy and not to trouble the police with these imaginings of his, but they cannot stop him. The man is stubborn, unreasonable, and obstinate. He calls the embassy and immediately afterward falls into a drunken stupor.

The manager is philosophical about it. It's sad that the timing should be so bad. After all, Erridge could just as well have done his passing out before he made that call instead of immediately after, but it was understandable. Having done what he is drunkenly determined to do, Erridge is satisfied. He allows himself to relax, and that's the way it is with drunks. Once they allow themselves to relax, the alcohol does the rest.

They're bearing no grudge. Mr. Erridge is more to be pitied than censured. They're taking it big. They're even so ready to give Mr. Erridge the benefit of the doubt that they now think he isn't at all the sort of cat who'd take up with the likes of Leonidas. It's their opinion that even that was an error attributable to drink.

I'll say this much for the gentlemen officers. They don't just leave it that way. They do ask questions, but from where Erridge sits, they don't seem quite the best questions, and they don't ask nearly enough of them. Riding back to their headquarters with them, I tell them what I think. I show them, lie by lie, how Paul and the manager have been snowing them.

The fuzz don't contradict me. They just remark on the great respectability of the Queen's Palace Hotel and on the impeccable records and reputations of every member of its staff. They dig how it must look to me, but just as my experience at the desk of the Axilles had seemed inexplicable, and that had been satisfactorily explained, similarly what had seemed to me inexplicable at the Queen's Palace had now also been satisfactorily explained.

"Who's going to explain how I got from one hotel to the other?" I growl.

They're working on that. For the rest of the time till we get to headquarters they're telling me that they have a record on

Constantine Leonidas. They concede that it may be hard for
Erridge to comprehend it, but they can understand how the
hotel people jumped to conclusions about Erridge. A man, of
whom you know nothing, evidences a strong yen to join up
with a cat about whom you know all too much and all of that
bad. What are you to think?

So I'm down to the analysis of whatever the lab will find dried
on to that whiskey glass and a hope that the pattern is going
to break down with the hackie. How can he possibly dream up
a convincing lie for Erridge's peculiar passage from the Axilles
to the Queen's Palace?

Back at headquarters they've got everything waiting for us.
They've brought the hackie in, and the policeman has reported
as ordered. We have the cop in first. Since with him the Q and A
has to be in Greek, I get to use my embassy interpreter.

Yes, he remembers the American gentleman. He remembers
the episode. The cab was stopped because the passenger was
driving it, and the hackie was sitting idly beside him. This is un-
usual. It is also against the regulations. The hackie had explained that he'd been taken ill. He had spots before his eyes.
He couldn't drive. The passenger had kindly taken over in the
emergency. Americans are like that, kind and excellent drivers.
The passenger is in a hurry to get to the Queen's Palace Hotel.
When they get there, the hackie is hoping the spots will have
passed off enough so he can take over and pack his cab in for the
night.

A foreign visitor who can't even speak Greek certainly can't
be permitted to drive a taxi through the streets of Athens. It's
obvious that the gentleman lacks a proper Athenian hack license.
The cop took over and drove the cab to the Queen's Palace
Hotel. Yes, he did recall that the gentleman noted down the
medallion number of the cab and also his shield number.

No, he hadn't thought it peculiar. Wouldn't the gentleman be
thinking he had broken the law in driving the cab? Wouldn't he
want witnesses in case of trouble over his infraction of the laws
of the city of Athens?

I can't pick holes in any of that. What does this cop know except what he got by way of translation? From the first I hadn't for a moment believed that anything I said was being put into Greek for him, not when the translating was being done by the hackie, the doorman, and the Queen's Palace manager. The hackie was the one who'd have to come up with the answers. They bring the hackie in. The cop takes one look at him. I take one look at him. The cop explodes in Greek. I explode in English. There's no difference between us but language. We're both saying it's the wrong man. This one is short and skinny. He's old enough to be spots-before-the-eyes's father. Also this one speaks no English.

He hadn't worked the night before. He'd been taken ill. It was something he'd eaten. He'd gone home, parked his cab in the street outside his house, taken a cathartic, and gone to bed. My interpreter Englished every last word of it for me, even to the name and address of the old herb woman out toward Eleusis who supplied the cathartic. She concocted it from an ancient formula that came down to her all the way from Aesculepius himself. It wasn't any of the Turkish poison or German poison you can get in a drugstore.

The little, old man spits twice, and my interpreter explains that it's after he says Turkish and after he says German. That's to clear his mouth of any infection that's maybe been left there by the passage of the names across his tongue.

So he was out of action, but some misbegotten son of a Turk had used his cab during the night. Somebody had taken this precious vehicle which was all that stood between him and star-vation and had gone joyriding in it. When he had come out this morning, completely cured by his night with the Eleusinian mystery, the hack had been at the curb just where he'd left it the day before, but the gas was noticeably lower than it should have been, and there were more kilometers recorded on his speed-ometer than there should have been. If the gentlemen of the police could only catch this miscreant who robs a poor man of gasoline, if they could only lay by the heels this rascal who put unremunerated wear and tear on a poor man's already worn and torn hack, there would be one cabbie in Athens who ever after would pull up at every intersection to bless every traffic cop in town.

"Can he give us any sort of a clue to the cab thief?"

The question insults him. What manner of man do they take him for? If he himself had any way of finding this byblow of a long line of Turkish fathers, what could he want of the police?

The old boy is escorted out, and they have at the cop again. Now they want to know what happened after I was delivered at the Queen's Palace. Nothing happened. The cabbie suddenly was feeling a lot better. He wasn't seeing the spots any more. The cop rode with him while the hackie got his cab out of the maelstrom that boils through the avenue in front of the Queen's Palace. By the time the hackie drove him back to his beat, the fuzz was convinced that the man was back in full control and could be safely allowed to carry on alone.

And that's the whole of it. Nobody's asking why he didn't look at any driver's licenses. It's too bad he didn't know he had a car thief, but how was he to have known? It seems to Erridge that this is no way to run a fuzzorium, but what can I do about that? I have another point to make.

"We still have no answer on how I got from one hotel to the other," I say, "and as long as that's unexplained, none of the other explanations stand up either."

They disagree. All the explanations satisfy them. This in-between bit, they grant me, is still troublesome, but they'll leave no stone unturned. They'll find the cab thief. They'll have an explanation for that, too. They suggest that I forget the whole thing. All of Greece lies before me. I have seen none of the glories. I haven't been up on the Acropolis. I haven't been to the National Museum. There's Delphi and Olympia and Epidaurus and Corinth and Sounion and Aegina and Mycenae and Hydra. If I leave their country without taking a Greek Islands cruise, I'll never forgive myself.

"You haven't tasted *retsina* yet," they tell me. "Relax, Mr. Erridge," they urge. "Go get yourself a fix and relax."

Maybe I just went away from there. Maybe the interpreter led me out to Mom's hired car. I was in a state of shock. You know this cat, Erridge. With him it's always been live nine lives and let live nine lives. He's no blue-nosed type, but fuzz is fuzz and you expect it to go through the motions. "Go get yourself a fix." What kind of advice is that for high police brass to give a foreign visitor?

By the time I've driven around to the embassy and dropped the interpreter off, I've come to conclusions. I've done every last thing anybody can expect of a law-abiding cat. The fuzz can take it from here. Erridge is through with it.

One of the things I'd learned from the police was that the dead man was an Egyptian named Hamid, newly arrived from Cairo. He was carrying an Egyptian passport and the date of entry stamped on it was the day he died. The records showed his flight number and time of arrival. He'd beat Erridge into Athens by half a day, coming over on a morning plane.

Back at the Queen's Palace I asked the doorman where I could leave the car. He said he'd take care of it for me. I told him not to take it too far away till I knew whether we'd be wanting it any more that evening. I was easing myself back into the role I'd planned for myself at the beginning. For as long as I was in Greece I was going to be nothing but Mom's Matthew. Whatever plans she had, I was going to be at her disposal.

"I'll just park it around the corner for you, sir," the doorman said. "Mrs. Erridge told me you'll be needing it this evening."

"Right. Then keep it handy."

At his desk in the lobby Paul was putting the whole man into the job of sticking stamps on picture postcards. He couldn't have been more completely occupied if he'd been hanging wallpaper. I didn't disturb him. The manager wasn't in evidence and I didn't go looking for him. Upstairs Mom was in her room with the connecting door open. She called to me.

"Matthew," she said.

"At your service, kid."

She came to the door and looked at me. "Are you all right?"

"Never righter."

On the floor beside the luggage rack where my bag sat there was another one. It had my initials on it, and it was brand new. I was looking at it. Mom was watching me.

"I'd have had you all packed, but you left your bag locked, and I couldn't get at your things."

"We going somewhere?" I asked.

"As soon as you're packed. Mrs. Grymm and I have finished ours."

"Where are we going?"

"A place at the shore, down on the Peloponnese. Mrs. Grymm has been there. She says it's heaven."

"The doorman said we'll be wanting the car."

"Yes. I told him. I know you've never minded night driving, and Mrs. Grymm knows the road. She says it's good all the way."

"I don't mind, but isn't there stuff you'll want to see en route. It'll be dark before we're out of here."

"I know, but since we have to move anyhow."

"Have to move?"

"Yes. The manager told me when I came in. They need these two rooms. People coming tonight had them reserved for months."

"No other rooms they can give us?"

She went through the song and dance they'd handed her. People occupying two choice rooms had been due to check out at noon. Lady fell ill. Doctor confined her to her bed. Naturally they can't be asked to move and now with these others coming in with confirmed reservations, and so on.

"It's because of me," I said.

"Obviously," Mom agreed, "and completely unwarranted. It's not as though you made a public spectacle of yourself. It can't be the first time a guest slept late. Whether you were tired or had been drinking too much is no business of theirs. I must say I'm disappointed in them, and Mrs. Grymm is furious."

"They ask for her room too?"

"No, but she feels it's a poor way to treat people who are here on her recommendation. She told the manager it was an outrage, and he could have her room as well."

There'd be no problem about rooms at the place down on the shore. Mrs. Grymm had made telephone reservations, and she had a promise that we could stay as long as we liked.

"It's not like Athens hotels," Mom explained. "It's off the beaten track for the ordinary sort of tourist."

A little shame-facedly Mom confessed that she had coaxed Mrs. Grymm into coming along with us to this new place.

"I hadn't begun to get over the shock of being asked to leave the hotel," Mom said. "After all, this is a new experience for me, being thrown out of a place."

"I'm sorry about that," I said.

"Don't be silly. That manager is being completely unreasonable, but I wouldn't have known what to do or where to go, and you can't imagine how comforting it was to have someone simply take the whole thing into her hands. She suggested this place I've been wanting to go to anyway, and she telephoned down there and fixed the rooms up and everything, and all of that while I was still dithering. Matthew, just seeing her being so calm and practical about everything, even when she was furious with the hotel, and then hearing her on the telephone handling the Greek so well, I was overcome with the feeling that we'd never be able to manage at all without her. The Greeks are so peculiar. While we were waiting for her call to go through, I'm afraid I broke down and begged her to come with us. And you know, dear, she couldn't have been sweeter about it. All that was bothering her was that she might be in the way, that I'd rather go off alone with you."

"Isn't this sudden change gumming up her plans?" I asked.

"She's lonely, the poor dear. I'm certain she's had no plans at all except hoping she might find someone she could go about with. Loneliness is a dreadful thing, Matthew."

"Okay," I said. "Let's give her a ball."

It was a load off Mom's mind. She pushed me back to my packing.

"Where'd the new bag come from?" I asked.

"I bought it for you. Yours has a disgusting looking stain on the leather. The new one's a present. Pack it quickly, Matthew. Let's be out of here."

I got at the repacking. In the old bag I came on the whiskey, the bottle Guido and I had nicked on the way in to Cairo. It reminded me. The other bottle was gone from the bedside table.

"What happened to the rest of the booze?" I asked.

Mom fought down a look of distress. "Mrs. Grymm and I finished it before we started packing," she said. "We were so angry. We needed something to settle us down."

Going on with the packing, I left the whiskey where it lay. I was thinking I hadn't had a single drink all day, and then I tried to remember when I'd last eaten. The coffee Mom gave me to wake up on. The nuts I bought from the man with the attaché case. The meal on the plane had looked like a TV dinner Cleopatra maybe had hotted up for Anthony and he hadn't gotten around to eating it. I'd passed that up, thinking that first thing in Athens I'd be taking Mom out to the best place in town.

"You know," I said thoughtfully. "I've had a busy afternoon. I forgot all about eating. Nothing all day."

Mom was horrified. She'd do my packing while I called room service for something to eat.

"Here?" I said. "I'll go on a hunger strike first."

I was thinking about mickeys, but Mom took it for resentment. She called Mrs. Grymm. We'd be ready to take off almost immediately, but could we stop for dinner on our way out of town even if it did make us very late getting down to the Peloponnese? Matthew hadn't eaten all day.

She came away from the phone. It was all set. Mrs. Grymm was calling the Dionysus to reserve a table.

"Dionysus?" I said. "Maenads. Satyrs. Isn't it wild?"

Mom laughed. "It's the best place here," she said.

The getaway from the hotel is a record breaker. Nobody around to say any goodbys, but bills are ready, car is at door, platoons of bellhops load our stuff.

Mrs. Grymm tells me how to go. She knows her way around even to what streets are one-way and which way. We cross the square with the pepper trees in it and head down a broad avenue that runs alongside the park. When the Jupiter temple comes up on our left, we take a right turn. The town is at its liveliest. All the stores are open, and the streets are full of people. It's one of those towns where everything closes from one to four and then the stores are jumping till eight or nine at night.

I'm trying to keep my mind on driving and seeing the sights, but it keeps going back to the sights I'd seen just as I was pulling us away from the hotel. Across the avenue, out in front of the cafe, a pair of cats in a huddle. One had the attaché case, and I knew him on sight, the lad who'd sold me the hazelnuts. He was huddling with Constantine Leonidas, the disreputable Spartan.

I had a short-lived impulse to pop across and collar Leonidas, but I let it die. The fuzz were looking for him. They'd made it clear that they knew their work better than Erridge did. Why should I do their job for them? I didn't feel that much in their debt.

The cafe was doing business. Several tables were occupied, and at three I spotted familiar faces. One gentleman, looking smaller than he did at home because he wasn't wearing his flowing robes, sat alone at one table. At each of the tables either side of him sat two men. Since they hadn't changed into European clothes, they looked as they always had, complete with revolvers, dirks, and bandoliers of revolver shells. It was my son of the desert, flanked by the trusted inner cadre of his bodyguard. If I had gone to collar Kostya, these friends from the south would have had front-row seats for the show. At least half of my reason for being in Athens was needing a vacation from these babies.

Also there were ladies present. Just at the moment I saw all these old buddies, Grymm was in the process of telling me which way to go, and Mom broke in on her, which was uncharacteristic.

"Get going, Matt," she said. "It doesn't matter which way. Just get us away from here."

As I'm driving, I keep wondering about that. I know she's gone off the hotel. I know she's worried about her boy's empty gut, but it just doesn't seem enough. Mom never interrupts, even when she's at her most impatient.

It wasn't that she'd also caught sight of Kostya or of the Sonof. They wouldn't mean a thing to her, and anyhow she was looking the other way.

We're held up by a traffic light right in front of a little store that has its show window stacked full of weapons. Rifles, shot-guns, pistols, revolvers, hunting knives, fish-gutting knives, shivs, harpoons, saps, billy clubs, sword canes, and hand grenades. I feel in my pocket for Leonidas's worry beads.

"Mom," I say. "What was bugging you back at the hotel?"

"Bugging me?"

That's Mom. Mostly she digs me all right, but she hopes that by making me translate into her kind of English, she'll maybe lure me back to the words I learned at her knee. I let her have an earful of those.

"What transpired in front of the hotel to precipitate extreme perturbation."

"That's worse," Mom giggles, "because it's pompous. It's the silliest thing. I saw my policeman. He wasn't in uniform, but I recognized him."

"The one with the paws?" I ask.

"The filthy brute," Grymm contributes.

"I'd like to meet him."

"Drive on, Matthew. You need your dinner."

We pass the Theater of Dionysus and then the Roman one, the Herod Atticus. Grymm and Mom know them all, and they call them by name. Hanging over the theaters and over us, there's the Acropolis. I recognize the Parthenon in the moonlight, but Mom makes a point of calling my attention to its beautiful little sister. It's the Temple of the *Nike Apteros,* the Victory without Wings. My babe with the clinging chiffon came off that one.

I want to ask Mom where the titmouse lives, but I remember Grymm in the back seat. I can see her in the rear-view mirror. She's wearing her white gloves and her hairnet, and I can see she's still thinking about Mom's fuzz. She's got that pickles-won't-melt-in-her-mouth look. Just opposite the Acropolis she tells me to turn left.

The restaurant is right there across the road. It's as new as the Parthenon is old. The whole front of it is glass, and inside it's no more lit up than the bar back at the QP. You can just make out the tables with their white cloths and waiters drifting back and forth behind their white shirt fronts.

You know the four eras of restaurant lighting. Go back far enough, and they were lit by oil lamps and candles. Then came gaslight. Then electricity, and you could tell cream from ketchup. Now we're in the fourth era, *crepe suzette* lighting. All you get to see by is the light thrown out by the flaming brandy.

A waiter captain with cat's eyes led us to a table right up against the glass, and I'll say this for the Dionysus, giving you a grandstand seat for the moon-bathed Acropolis, they weren't going to compete with it by letting you look at your food.

I dug right off it was an everything-cooked-to-order beanery. I settled the ladies at the table and promptly excused myself. I had a quick errand to do. I'd be back by the time the food would be coming up. I asked Mom to order for me.

"Must you?" she sighed.

A busboy was dealing out rolls. Mom pressed one into my hand. I promised I'd eat it to hold me till I got back. I kept the promise and wished it had been two rolls, or better still a half a dozen. Grymm went out toward the door with me. She wanted a phone booth, an insurance call to tell our new hotel we'd be even later than she'd said.

I left her to it and galloped out to the parking lot. On my

way to the car I turned to blow Mom a kiss. I couldn't see her, but I knew she was there. Someone back in the restaurant had a flashlight. It could be handy for finding your plate, but this flashlight was being put to another use. It went on and off in sequences of longs and shorts. Without stopping to think that reading the Morse wouldn't be any good to me since it would be in Greek, I took it in automatically. A short, two longs, and a short. Three longs. Two shorts and a long.

It stopped with that. I climbed in the car and took off. Driving back past the Acropolis, I ran the groups through my head. I'd picked up only the finish, of course, and it was no better than I'd expected it to be. It had to be international Morse, and it read for "*pou.*"

I drove back to the gun shop we'd passed. I liked the little sign on the door: ENGLISH SPOKEN HERE. Better still, the English speaker had to be called out of the back room, and she was a great improvement on the man who first came forward to serve me. I wondered wistfully why Mom couldn't have taken up with her instead of with Mrs. Grymm. She was just as proficient at the Greek-English bit, and there was nothing to separate her from the honey cake who tied her sandal back in my room at the QP except a matter of some twenty-five hundred years. What she wore was only clingy enough to suggest what the babe in the picture revealed, but let's be reasonable, Charlie. To be waited on in a gun store by a beautiful little baklava who's wearing something that shapes her wherever she's there to be shaped, may not be enough, but it's all you're ever going to get. You can't ask for the single layer of soaking wet chiffon. The water would rust the guns.

Suddenly it came over me that for at least forty-eight hours I'd been forgetting it was spring. She asked me what she could do for me, and, making the big effort, I brought it down to the paltry bit I'd had in mind when I came in. I wanted a hand gun and a supply of ammo for it.

She took her time looking me over, and I had the feeling that, if I was comparing her with that picture back in my hotel room, she was comparing me with those studs in the pictures in the room Mom had.

"I have just what you want," she said, as though I had to be told; but however little she sounded like it, she was talking about firearms. She dug under the counter and came up with a husky .45.

"Nice," I said, "but much too big."

Looking me over again, she gave me an argument. "It's a lot of revolver for a lot of man," she said.

"Thanks," I said. "Anywhere I carry that, it's going to make my clothes bulge. Brioni won't like it. He's my tailor."

Setting the .45 aside, she walked around me slowly. I liked what she did with her hips, which was just as well because I could concentrate on that and not think too much about what she was doing with her eyes. Even when she came around behind where I couldn't see her, I felt her look travel over me. I know that you don't ever feel X rays at all, but it was how X rays ought to feel—penetrating.

"What you need then," she said, "will depend on where you want to carry it. You can't carry it where I keep mine."

She had a gold chain around her neck, thick and heavy, about like her little finger. I hadn't seen one like that on a dame before, but in even the short time I'd had for Athens sightseeing, I'd noticed a couple of men who were wearing them. They were priests, and they hung big pectoral crosses from their chains.

Hers hung down inside her dress. With a little, husky laugh she hauled up on her hawser and fetched up out of its lair one of those neat, little automatics that look like a toy, but only to cats who've never looked one in the eye. It's no big slug those things throw; but aim one right, and it's just as lethal as it needs to be.

She fished it up just far enough to let me see what it was, and then she dropped it back in. It asked for gallantry.

"That pistol," I said, "must be the envy of every man in .thens."

"We'll find you one that'll be the envy of every woman," she said. "Take off your coat and shirt."

I had ideas about what she might take off; but, in that store behind a show window that had a couple of really nosy noses pressed against it, I left my ideas unspoken. She brought out as pretty a rig as a man could want. It was a shoulder holster made of soft, light leather in thongs so thin you'd think they didn't have enough heft to support the weight of a kid's plastic water pistol. What she brought up to go with it was no water pistol. It was a flat, short-barreled automatic, so neat and compact that it made the .45 look like a howitzer, but substantially bigger than the nasty little thing that inhabited the living space that was so much better than it deserved.

I took my coat off and reached. She did the upward nod. "Your shirt, too," she said. "We fit these right to your skin." So I took my shirt off. "When I sweat," I asked, "won't it foul the gun?"

"The holster," she said, "is waterproof, and as long as a man feels this hugging him, he has nothing to sweat about."

The fitting went quickly, much too quickly. Maybe I'll never again feel anything as smooth, as soft, or as cool as the touch of her hands against my skin until maybe they lay a lily on my chest. Maybe I should put it in my will—bury me with my shirt off and a lily on my chest.

When she finished, the pistol sat flat against my ribs under my left arm, and the harness held it firm and steady. It was comfortable. It felt secure, and it didn't bulge or knot anywhere. I took a big breath. I swung my arms. I flexed my shoulders. No constriction anywhere. I drew the pistol out of the holster. It hung in such nice balance that it seemed to jump into my hand. She picked up my shirt.

"Try drawing it with your clothes on," she said, sounding regretful.

I reached for my shirt, but she kept hold of it, and she put it on me. We should have been doing this in the back room, but I'd used up too much of my time already. She buttoned my shirt, but she let me tie my own tie. She showed me how to leave two buttons open under the tie for times when I might have to go in there for a quick draw. Then she helped me into my coat.

I tried drawing the gun. It worked fine. She produced a box of ammo while I was checking the mechanism. It might have been made for me. Perfect tension on the trigger spring, everything just right. I rammed a clip into it and returned it to the holster. Then I looked at myself in the mirror. Nothing to show I was heeled. Even under Mom's penetrating eye I was going to get away with it. All I had to do was tuck my shirttails in, and I was all set.

Before I'd more than started on the shirttails, the girl closed in and pushed my hands away. She did them for me. If that baby didn't dig customer service, it's never been dug. More to take my mind off it than anything else, I asked her what I owed her.

All right, so she looked disappointed in me. I was disappointed in myself. It's better that it should never happen to a man at all than for it to happen just at dinnertime. With every evidence of regret on both sides, the transaction was completed with nothing but drachma. She wrapped my extra ammo for me; and when I said something about coming back another day when I'd have more time, she answered politely enough, but she was looking at me now like I might have been Kostya Leonidas.

Driving back to the Dionysus, I was thinking I could have asked the girl what "*pou*" meant, but it had completely left my mind. It didn't matter. I could ask Mrs. Grymm.

The traffic was thinning out a little. I had a quick and easy ride back. As I approached the table, a waiter lifted a plate of cold lobster off a bed of ice. With one hand he pulled my chair out for me. With the other he slipped the lobster in front of me.

"Eat that up, Matthew," Mom told me. "I ordered you some of this lamb and eggplant to follow."

Mom and Mrs. Grymm were on their lamb and eggplant, and

they were having beer with it. The waiter poured one out for me.

Mrs. Grymm was apologizing for not having tagged along with me just in case of any trouble with the language.

"It was easy," I said. "They spoke English, but what does 'pow' mean?"

"Pow?" She looked bewildered.

"Maybe it isn't Greek," I said.

"How do you spell it?"

"P-O-U."

"Oh," she said, repeating it after me. "It means 'where.' Do you remember the rest of the sentence?"

"No. Only the one word."

She laughed. "You're learning the language anyhow," she said, "even if it's only one word at a time. You don't pronounce it 'pow.' It's 'poo.'"

"As in Winnie the . . ." Mom added.

I was well into my lobster, and I took a drag on my beer, finding both surprisingly good. Mom was watching me, and her pleasure was showing.

"The Greek wines are disappointing," she said. "The retsina tastes like turpentine, and unresinated they taste like nothing at all. I've taken to having a fix instead. That's why I ordered you one."

"You must be kidding?"

Mom looked anxious. "Aren't you enjoying it?" she asked.

The waiter came up to pour me some more beer. I could read the label on the bottle. For some reason it wasn't in Greek letters; and there it was, spelling it right out—F-I-X, fix. Just that one little item made me feel a lot better about everything, even about the Athenian fuzz.

VIII

We left Athens by the western road, through Daphne and Eleusis, and Grymm was full of how we'd have to come back by daylight so we could see it. We went bowling past docks and tankers and oil refineries while Grymm went on and on, talking about what lay around us, as though twenty-five centuries had never happened.

Those freight piers rimmed the Saronic Gulf, and out there lay Salamis where the Athenian ships knocked off the Persian fleet. Daphne was Byzantine mosaics, and Eleusis was the place of the mysteries. I was thinking, "and of cathartics," but she talked like a guide book, and I wondered which one she'd been memorizing.

As you must have dug by now, Erridge is no Greek expert; but I've kicked around the Mediterranean, and stuff has seeped in. Let's say I've got an ear for the phony. The lady knew from nothing. She was feeding us dull inaccuracies she'd picked up from some tourist guide.

I kept reminding myself that for the interpreting bit she was great, but the babe in the gun shop would have done every bit as well with that, and she could never have been dull.

I told myself again and again that Grymm was along because Mom wanted her and that I owed Mom at least that much after having brought to her the new experience of being booted out of a hotel. Also substituting the gunshop baklava for Grymm was a dream of bliss, but what was to say I could ever have lured the luscious tomato away from her arsenal?

Once we'd cleared Eleusis, we were out of the city, and I started pushing hard. Remember I'm driving the silly heap the car-hire people handed Mom. I was getting out of it all the speed it had; and if I needed anything to tell me that wasn't much, there was the Citroën.

Any time I'm on my own wheels, it's different. Mine is a Porsche, and there's nothing I've ever asked of it that it couldn't do. It runs by reading my mind. We leave even the most hopped-up Citroëns for dead.

I had the accelerator pushing a hole through the floor boards, and the way that Citroën went past me I could have been pulled up taking on gas. You drive a heap that drags like that, and first thing you know it's like all your weight is going up into your eyelids.

To make it worse, Grymm goes on and on with the phony guidebook spiel. Up ahead lies Corinth, and past there we'll be turning left, heading south through the Argolid. Argos and Tiryns are going to be on our road. Off on a little spur we won't be taking that night lies Mycenae, and Grymm tells me about how Agamemnon came home from sacking Troy and never got past his first bath. That's a great story about how his wife, Clytemnestra, got together with her lover and scrubbed the old boy, but if it's going to keep you awake, you want to hear it the way Aeschylus told it and not as told by Mrs. Grymm.

Coming up on Corinth, we hit a roadside *taverna* that's going full blast. Twanging *bazoukis*, full throated singing, jumping-up-and-down dancing, food and drink. I pull up.

"Coffee to keep me awake," I say.

Mom offers to spell me on the driving, but her eyelids look heavier than mine, and I tell her I don't need anything but coffee and a leg stretch. The Citroën is parked outside the taverna, and a couple of young cats are in the back seat of it eating bread and cheese and tomatoes. They're heavy on hair and

heavy on beard which can, of course, be their way of making
the scene except that somehow they haven't the look.

They give us a cheery *kalispera*, and their Greek sounds real
good. Inside the spot is jumping, but we get quick service on
our coffee. The music is loud enough to wake the dead, and
monotonous enough to put them back to sleep again. These
people know only one tune and they do it over and over again
indefinitely. The tune has been played too much. The air has
been breathed too much. Sitting there is doing me no good. I
order a second round of coffees, and, leaving Mom and Grymm
at the table, I carry mine outside.

The kids have come out of the Citroën. They're over by
Mom's hired heap, examining it closely. Seeing them out in the
open, I'm getting a fuller picture. They're big, husky, and ragged.
They couldn't have been wearing less. Even in Greece you've got
to be marble or bronze to go around totally barebutt. They had
on sandals that were nothing but soles and a thong that came
up inside the big toe and looped around the ankle. Their short
shorts were even shorter from having frayed out at the bottom.
The sleeves of their shirts had also frayed away clear up to their
shoulders, and they were holding them together by tying the
shirt tails in front. This has long been a style around the beaches
in hot countries, but on these huskies it obviously wasn't style.
They had run out of buttons.

Since they had a Citroën that could leave our job like standing
still, it doesn't seem likely that they'll be thinking of jumping
the ignition on the heap and making off with it, but I stroll
over there just in case. They see me coming. They're all grins and
innocence.

"Hi," they say this time.

"Hi."

"You're American, aren't you?"

"Nothing else, Charlie."

"Us, too."

They seem friendly, but I've been tangling with too many
strangers. I'm playing it cool.

"It's a small world," I say.

Both of them have brown hair, but the beards are different. On one it's come out pink. On the other it's russet.

"Maybe it's getting too small," says russet beard.

"Maybe, man, it's getting so you're feeling like a little crowded," says pink beard.

Innuendo I don't need. "Who's crowding me?" I ask.

"I'm Roy," pink beard tells me, offering his hand.

I look at it before I shake. I have to see if all that is hand, or if maybe he's forgotten to take off his catcher's mitt. It's all hand. We shake.

"I'm Matt," I tell him.

So now we know each other, and he can introduce russet beard. He's Jake. Jake is smaller, but only like Heracles is maybe smaller than Atlas.

"We're wondering like whether you know there's these cats have a tail on you," Jake remarks.

It's friendly, and it's cool. He might be calling my attention to a radiator leak or a crankcase drip.

"What breed of cat?" I ask.

They look at each other and shrug. "Like Turks maybe," Roy offers.

"Talking to each other," Jake adds. "It isn't Greek, but we stop there. We don't know Turkish from Armenian or Arabic, but it's like that. East of Suez stuff; and if they don't talk Kipling, they lose us."

"They're gone now," Roy tells me, "but they did stop, and they all got out and cased your car. They saw us watching, and maybe that's why they only looked. Then the fuzz came along and pulled up there across the road. That kicked it over. Those babies piled back into their car and took off quick like. We're figuring they'll be waiting for you some place up ahead, them and the other Cadillac full of the same that didn't stop."

I looked across the road where they indicated police. It's a car parked in the shadows, and it's not showing any lights.

"You're sure that one's fuzz?" I ask.

"We've been over there talking to them. We asked them about the roads, just to check. They're local fuzz."

It's to think about. The way the kids tell it, these other cats, at sight of the uniforms, pile back in their Cadillac and take off. Are they followed? They are not. So what's the fuzz doing sitting in the dark across the road? Holding hands or keeping an eye on Erridge?

"Two Caddies," I say, "and you thought they were both following me?"

They're polite about it, but not too polite to make themselves clear. They're giving me credit for being hep enough to know that the thing I'm driving won't do anything at Indianapolis. It's nothing I'm doing to it that makes it drag its tail. What can you expect from the heap? It's the model that came in after the oxcart. I've got to expect that I'll be living in everybody's exhaust. It isn't like I'm driving a couple of latest model, super-de-luxe Cadillacs.

"You know how we passed you in that frog terrine we been riding," Jake says.

"How come the Corinthian jerk who's been driving us can get up enough steam in that cruddy *bain-marie* of his so he takes all three the same way—the two Caddies and you—zip, zip, and zip like you were all running in reverse?" Roy elaborates.

"Nice of you to tip me," I say, winding up to thank them.

They cut across my thank yous. "At least some of our motives were ulterior, Matt," Jake tells me.

"Like what?"

"Like you give us a lift, Matt."

"Where to?"

"Wherever you're going, so long as it's out of Corinth."

"You hot here in Corinth?"

They assure me that they're not hot anywhere. It's just that they've been to Corinth before, and they've seen everything Corinth has to show, and their lift in the Citroën is good for only other five kilometers. They're riding with a Corinthian, and 's almost home.

"If he liked his wife's cooking," Jake explains, "he'd be home by now."

"We can spell you with the driving," Roy urges.

"Suppose I'm going some place you've already been?"

That's not worrying them. There's no place up ahead that they don't like except maybe Patras, and they like that better than Corinth. Otherwise out there on the Peloponnese it's all stuff they're glad to go back to or new spots they're wanting to see.

"We're great drivers," Jake assures me. "If it's got wheels, we can roll it. Also leave us not forget two Caddies loaded with cats. You find yourself a rumble, we'll be more use to you than the ladies."

"I don't know," I tell them, "and you'll also need their okay."

"You just decide," Roy coaxes. "To ladies we're irresistible."

"It's because we're such clean-cut, American youths," Jake explains.

"Clean enough," I tell them, "but cut? It doesn't show."

I half expect they'll ask me what I've got against hair, but that's not the way they're playing it. The last razor blade is hopelessly blunted, and haircuts take bread which they haven't got to spare. But ladies are perceptive about stuff like that. They'll see at a glance that underneath it all Jake and Roy are as clean-cut as an American youth can be.

"We'll sweep them off their feet," Roy promises.

"It's our unbeatable combo," Jake adds. "We're both cute and dependable. You can't hope to dig us the way dames do."

"All right. If it's okay with them, but I make the rules."

They think that's fair enough, and they listen quietly while I'm lining it out. I have no reason for not trusting them, but I have no reason for trusting them either, and I'm not in a trusting mood. If I like the way they drive, and neither Grymm nor Mom minds, they can have their lift.

"You're going to be in front of me all the time," I tell them "and I'm going to have my eye on you all the time. First mo I don't like, I don't wait for you to make a second. You're ou

I slip my hand inside my shirt, and I produce the little automatic.

"The ladies?" Jake asks. "They heeled, too."

"No, and they don't know I am. I keep it that way unless I have to use it while they're around. They don't know I need this. They don't know we've been tailed. They know from nothing. Dig?"

Roy looks me over. Maybe I'm asking a favor of him, and he's weighing it up, whether he'll play a long with me or not.

"Could be you're not giving them a fair shake," he says. "Could be you're hotter than Hephaestus's forge, and you're using the ladies for cover."

"One of them's my mother. The other is her friend. I've been in the country a little more than twenty-four hours. I've been kidnaped once, blipped on the head twice so I was laid out cold both times, drugged once, tailed constantly, and lied to all over the place. All this by crumbs I've never seen before and not a clue to who or why. So far it's all been on me. It hasn't spilled over on to Mom or her friend. I'm hell bent on keeping it that way. If you want to go look for someone else to ride with, that's the smart way to play it. I'm the wrong cat to know. Maybe I'm some kind of Typhoid Mary, except it isn't typhoid I'm carrying. It's violence and maybe sudden death."

"It's also kicks," Jake murmurs. "We see you, Matt, and we see the apes in those two Caddies. We don't like their looks, and we do like yours." He turns to Roy. "Right, Charlie?" he asks.

"Rightish," Roy mutters. "What I'm asking myself is why we do like his looks and not theirs. Because he's American and they're not? Americans can be finks like anybody else. We've learned that. No?"

Jake argues it. All I can make of it is they've been tangled with a couple of the finkiest rats ever to dig cheese. Jake is contending they never had the first doubt about that pair. They'd known them for rats from the start, and they'd snowed themselves into thinking they could live with it.

"So we learned," he says. "So we saw they were finkier than we could ever imagine. It was never a question of anything but how much."

Roy looks me over some more. "At first sight we could tell they had no fur on their tails," he concedes. "Matt does look okay."

I'm getting tired of it. I move to break it up. "I'm going in to get the ladies," I say. "You coming or are you finding yourselves another ride?"

Roy breaks out a grin. "In," he says. "We can take a chance on that crate you're driving, we can take a chance on you."

I take them inside and introduce them. They break out the kind of manners Mom spent the best years of her life trying to teach me. I explain to the gals that it's for them to decide.

Roy speaks up. "With Matt it's patriotism," he says. "He wants to get us out of plain sight on the road before Americans get a bad name."

Mom laughs; and I know she's sold before she even says a word. It's the way she looks at them, like they're a brace of puppies she wants to take around to the poodle shop for clipping and grooming. Grymm looks less happy about them, but Mom's speaking before Grymm can find herself any words.

"I'm at least as patriotic as Matthew," Mom says.

They turn to Grymm. "Ma'am?" they say.

"I should like to see your passports," she says.

They hand them over, and the way she scrutinizes them, it can be rubber stamps turn her on. She takes them page by page, deciphering the record of every border crossing they've made. At long last she hands the passports back.

"If Mrs. Erridge wants to take you along," she says, "I'll not object."

There's no warmth in it. She's bowing to a two-thirds vote.

"Thanks a million, ma'am," Roy says.

"We'll grow on you, ma'am," Jake promises.

They take off across the taverna to say goodby to their Corinthian. I watch, and if there's any more exchange with the man than just that, it doesn't show. Meanwhile Grymm is explaining her misgivings. Asking for the passports, she says, was just a device. Travelers don't like letting their passports out of their hands.

"You take someone's passport," Grymm says, "and all the time you have it, he'll stand as close to you as he can get. All that hair. It just didn't seem possible they would be uninfested. I did have typhus shots, but nevertheless."

"It is a thought," I concur.

"That's why I held their passports long enough to make them nervous," Grymm explains. "So they would edge closer and closer."

"You okayed them," I say. "Then you haven't begun to itch."

Mom shudders. "Matthew," she protests. "They're ragged and unkempt, but they are clean."

"Yes," Grymm agrees. "They smell clean."

So the kids took over on the driving, and I sat in the back with the ladies. The lead came out of the eyelids. I was wide eyed, sharp, observant, reflexes in good working order.

Even if Jake hadn't been whistling "I Love a Parade," I couldn't have missed the carload of fuzz when they brought their lights back on and followed so close behind us that it could have been they were thinking we wouldn't make it unless they gave us a push. With them crawling up our back there was no seeing anything that might be coming along behind them. That's why I don't know just how far we'd gone before we picked up the first of our Cadillacs.

The fuzz stayed with us straight through the town. It was only when we turned south into the open country that they let us pull away from them, and it was then I saw the other pair of road lights. This car, however, was keeping its distance. We weren't losing it, and it wasn't gaining on us. There was no telling what make car it was or who was in it, but unless we were being tailed in relays, this would have to be one of those Caddies Jake and Roy had reported.

This time I began whistling "I Love a Parade." Before I was through the first chorus, both Jake and Roy puckered up to

make it a trio. Out of nowhere had come another set of lights
to roll along in our wake. This car positioned itself just midway
between us and the car I'd spotted when the fuzz first dropped
away. Two Cadillacs? Nothing could have been more likely.

Both Mom and Grymm had left forwarding addresses on de-
parting the Queen's Palace. It was an easy guess that the management tipped the authorities to our departure and to where
we were headed. So the locals in towns we'd be hitting had
been alerted to our coming through. That much I could dig.
We'd had a police escort through Corinth. The local boys had
picked us up where we crossed the boundary into their jurisdic-
tion. They'd stayed with us till we'd crossed out of it.

It was the two cars that were still with us that wanted thinking about. The whole deal had Erridge bugged, but what was
bugging me most was knowing I was up against an intelligence
operation that was much too good. Like the night before—how
had that cabbie who was no cabbie known it was to the QP
Mom had moved? Now we had it all over again. I could dig
the fuzz knowing we'd left Athens and where for, but these cats
in the Cadillacs also knew. At least one of the cars had gone on
through Corinth and turned down the southbound road to wait
for us there. They'd known it was the road we'd be taking. It
wasn't something they could have figured. If we were touring,
this road down to the Argolid isn't the only one tourists take
when they cross on to the Peloponnese. Olympia lies straight on
to the west, and also to the west there's Patras and the car ferry
over to Brindisi.

Roy was at the wheel. He drew up at the side of the road and
got out and walked around the car, checking the tires like. Jake
slid across to take over the wheel. I didn't want to crane around
too much to see what the boys in the back room were doing,
because there was always the chance that Mom and Grymm
didn't know we had us a tail, and I had this feeling that kept
telling me their ignorance was my bliss.

I did venture a look back like I was only checking on what
Roy was doing. Keeping their carefully set intervals behind us,

the two cars had stopped when we stopped. Roy scrambled back into the car, and Jake set her rolling.

"Something about the way she seemed to move," Roy explained apologetically, "made me think we maybe had a shoe gone soft, but they're all okay."

"What you were feeling, Charlie," Jake purred, "must have been your head going soft. She's moving fine. For her anyhow, she's moving fine."

Pretending like the mere mention of possible rear tire trouble had me so bothered I had to look back for what I couldn't possibly see, I took a quick glance. It was as I expected. The two sets of headlights were again in motion. We'd lost no units out of our parade.

I could have been less sneaky. Grymm spoke up.

"I'm an inquisitive old woman," she said, "and I've been thinking. You two boys—aside from being short of funds—had better start telling us what other kinds of trouble you're in."

"All kinds, ma'am," Roy answered readily, "and most all of it hooked up to the shortage in the bread department."

"You're hungry," Mom wailed, quickly solicitous.

"Not right now, ma'am," Roy said.

"We ate while we were stopped back there in Corinth," Jake added.

Maybe Mom dug it, but anyhow I stepped in with a further explanation. Maybe Grymm would forget the next question I could see trembling on her lips.

"Bread," I said, "is the new word for money."

"Bread," Mom marveled. "I'd hardly come to know it was lettuce before people started saying bananas. Now it's bread."

"You can still say bananas, ma'am," Jake told her. "Lettuce, that's become pretty square."

"But you can never say money?" Mom asked. "If you let money mean money and bread mean bread and dig mean excavate and cat mean feline, you'd be easier to understand. Don't you think?"

The kids laughed. Roy dropped to a confidential whisper.

"Don't ever tell anyone I said it," he told her, "because it's ratting on my peer group. We don't want to be understood."

"I am square as well as inquisitive," Grymm said. "I am also observant. Leaving Corinth, we had a police escort to see us out of town. Since then we've had two cars following us all the way. Since we weren't getting all this attention before you boys joined us, we have a right to know whether your being followed arises from the fundamental shortage of bread or from other causes, and whichever way, we are also going to want to know what this is all about."

"Those two heaps back of us?" Jake asked.

"And the police car that saw us out of Corinth," Grymm persisted.

"It's the way Greeks feel about driving the country at night," Roy offered, "and it's the way Greeks feel about Americans."

It was an answer of sorts even though I could make no sense of it. Obviously it wouldn't satisfy Grymm, but also obviously Roy wasn't just playing for time. He seemed to know where he was taking it.

Grymm was waiting, and Roy kept talking. Everywhere he and Jake kept hearing tales about bandits who swooped down out of the hills, descended on travelers, and left them at the roadside with pockets picked and throats cut. The boys took no stock in these tales. They had thumbed their way all along from Mount Athens across Chalcidice to Thessalonika and on down from there virtually the whole north-south length of the country to the Peloponnese, and in all that travel they had encountered no bandits and met no motorist who had so much as even glimpsed a bandit.

"It's all a myth," he said, "but it gets us most of our rides."

The way Roy told it, Greeks who'd gone fat and soft drove the roads in terror, and they jumped at the chance of picking up a pair of young, able-bodied traveling companions.

"They figure we're bodyguards like," Roy explained. "If we weren't Americans they'd pass us right by, figuring us to be bandits, but Americans? How could an American ever be a bandit?"

"And those cars," Grymm insisted. "They're still following us."

"Of course, they are," Roy said cheerily. "It's the next best thing to giving Jake and me a hitch. It's like riding in a convoy."

"Come bandits," Jake said, picking it up from Roy, "they can yell for help, and if they're on our tail, they'll have plenty of help available."

Grymm sniffed. She wasn't that easy to snow. "And the police back in Corinth," she said. "Riding in their police car in their own city, what was the matter with them? Did it make them feel safer, having three able-bodied Americans on hand to protect them?"

Jake laughed and immoderately. Mrs. Grymm had made a great, big, fat, wonderful, funny joke. He was going to have to remember that one. It was a real knee slapper. He did his best, but Grymm just didn't look jocular. She sat there tight-lipped, smoothing her little white gloves, and waiting for Jake to control himself and come up with an answer.

It was Roy, however, who again stepped in and fielded her question. They'd been hoping we wouldn't notice the police car. The Greek fuzz were on a campaign to discourage hitchhiking. It happened in every city they hit. The fuzz always escorted them out of town.

"If, like tonight, we have a ride," he said, "they see us out to the city limits to make sure we aren't dropped off some place in town."

"They catch us thumbing anywhere in town," Jake added, "they ride us out to the city limits themselves. Anything so they're sure we're out of town."

It took care of Grymm and her questions. I wasn't ungrateful, but I was a little worried. I began asking myself if it wasn't all just a little bit too slick. Turn a couple of dumb kids loose in a country where they know from nothing, and maybe someone sharp comes along and takes them, but good. So they're stranded, out of funds. Then again it doesn't even have to be that someone's taken them. They're just not smart enough to count when it's in drachma, and they run through the bread too fast.

This, however, is no pair of dumb kids. These are real cool cats. How do they get to be so broke? Or are they? So I have all these questions I want to ask, but I don't have to. Grymm asks them for me. Maybe it's just motherly type interest, and maybe she's still checking up on them, but now she's sounding motherly, and Mom's taking a hand as well.

They get the kids talking about where they've been and what they've seen. They've been everywhere and seen everything. If it's in Greece, you just name it. They'd hit it. Then they began talking about the islands, and Grymm pounced.

"When you get to the coast," she said, "you hitch rides on yachts?"

I tried that one. "Fat Greeks on the water," I said, "are scared of pirates."

"We were paying our way then," Roy told her.

"That was before the bread ran out," Jake added.

They were still talking when Mom corked off. Grymm was made of sterner stuff. She never closed an eye, but she did stop with the questions. We rode on in silence so we wouldn't wake Mom. We came out of the hills, and after a short run along the shore, we hit the town. The whole place was dark and shut up. Even the street lights were off.

Coming into town, we lost our twin tail. Grymm commented on it. "Now," she said, "they get brave."

"No bandits in town," Roy told her.

"You'll be wanting the boat landing," Jake said.

"Who needs boating this time of night," I growled. "Any idea of where the hotel is?"

"The boat landing," Grymm ordered. She turned to explain it to me. "Our hotel is on an island."

I was wondering how much more travel Mom could take before she saw a bed. "How far?" I asked.

"No distance at all," Grymm answered.

"Great," Roy chortled. "No time at all to row over there, Matt, and you'll see it's worth it. Beautiful spot, and it's historical, too."

"You been there?" I asked.

"Back before the bread ran out," Roy answered, "we were over there for a drink and a meal. We didn't stay there. Even then it was too de luxe for us."

"Where are you sleeping tonight?"

"On the beach. We sleep out all the time."

"Come over to the island and sleep out over there," I said, making with the invitation.

"There's no out over there," Jake told me. "Big stone wall rises right at the water's edge. Everything inside the wall is the hotel, the whole island."

"Like Alcatraz maybe," I grumbled.

Mom was awake, and she giggled.

"It was originally a Turkish prison," Roy explained.

"Ever since I first heard about it," Mom said, "I've been planning to come here. After they stopped using it as a prison, it was a rest home for retired executioners. Everybody says it's quiet and peaceful and utterly beautiful."

What can a cat do but play along?

"How would the executioners ever get any rest if it wasn't," I said.

IX

Crazy, man, crazy; but Erridge liked the place. For a cat who wants to get away from it all, it was perfect. For a man who wants to get away from two carloads of unexplained pursuers, it was made to order.

It's an offshore island. There's no access except by boat, and around the whole perimeter of the island only one landing place. The walls of this prison or hotel or hangman's home are of stone. They are high and thick. All around the island they rise straight up out of the water, slick and smooth and windowless for a good two-thirds of their height.

The landing is a broad, stone platform, and it's the only place you can set a foot down outside that wall. Otherwise not even a toehold. Since we were expected, the great, bronze-bound, wooden door stood open; but as soon as they had the three of us and our luggage inside it, a pair of Titans in porter's aprons leaned their combined weights against that door, swung it shut, and rammed its cyclopean bolts into their sockets.

We were in a tunnel-like corridor with another such massive door at the far end of it. This one also stood open, and beyond it lay a moonlit garden. We were ushered through, and the porters shut and bolted the second door behind us. The garden was big, leafy and cool and sweetly scented. The lemons, the oranges, and the almonds were all in blossom.

Maybe you're thinking that it isn't likely that in a Turkish pokey the prisoners would have had it so good; but you've got to remember that there would be a lot to a Turkish prison that wouldn't have been for the prisoners. The prison part would all be below ground. Dungeons don't need light or air or garden outlooks. Those were reserved for the governor of the prison, for his seraglio, for his retinue. That was the way they did things. The underside of any palace was likely to be a prison. The topside of any prison was certain to be a palace. The hotel was set up in the palace part of the deal, and all the modern conveniences had been added, plumbing, elevator, phone in every room.

The rooms were at the top of the place. Outside ones had broad windows with a view over the water. Inside ones had balconies that overlooked the garden. Mom and Grymm were inside. I was across the corridor from them. I looked out across the water toward the town.

All over these days they floodlight the walls of ancient monuments, and this was a place that rated floodlights. It's quite a trick the way they do it, pouring soft light over the walls and stopping it short of the windows. No light was shining in; but leaning out of my window, I could see the light-washed wall fall away below me, slick and sheer all the way down to the water.

I came away from the window and prepared to relax. I turned off the lights. I could undress and get myself to bed by moonlight. I'd last seen my pursuers when they'd turned off toward the heights back of the town. They could be perched up there now with binoculars looking straight across at this big open window of mine. I could pull the curtains and shut them out, but that would shut out as well the little breeze had had picked up on its way to me the scent of the sea and of flowering trees and of more spicily scented herbal shrubs than I've ever known the names for.

I skinned out of my clothes and was down to nothing but the shoulder holster and the little pistol when the knock came at my door. I grabbed a robe and belted it around me before I opened up. It was Mom. Seeing a dark room, she drew back.

"I didn't know you were already in bed," she moaned.

"I wasn't."

"Then what are you doing in the dark?"

"Undressing, enjoying the moonlight."

"I brought you a nightcap," she said.

"You're a woman in a million."

"It was Mrs. Grymm. She brought me one and one for you."

"You are two women in a million," I said, putting my head back and knocking off my whole drink in one big gulp.

Mom left me, and I skinned out of my robe. Earlier I'd been debating whether I should sleep in that shoulder holster or just settle for keeping the pistol handy under my pillow. Now I was asking myself why I wasn't looking for bogeymen under the bed. Maybe there was trouble waiting for me across the water, but it was there, and I was here. I would deal with it when I came to it; but now it was, "Get loose, Erridge. You're alone, Charlie. Nobody's coming after you. This is Peaceville, Man, Peaceville."

Hauling out of the shoulder holster, I left it draped over the back of a chair with the pistol hanging in it. It was a beautiful bed. The linen sheets on it were cool and smelled of lavender. A cat, stretching himself the length of a bed like that, can't feel as though he needs any armament. I wondered why I'd ever felt a need for the little weapon except for remembering how much fun I'd had having the thing fitted.

Since I hadn't pulled the curtains, daylight came at me early; but I flopped over on my face and slept again. It felt like much later when I came awake enough to look at my watch. It said eight o'clock, but I felt too comfortably slept out for anything that early, and the sun looked to be too far up the sky. I rubbed my eyes because, if I was going to doubt anything, it was going to be them and not the timepiece. I'd been a long time relying on that watch. If anything ever goes awry with the clocks at Greenwich, they can reset them by Erridge's watch. It was saying precisely one minute and a half after eight.

I phoned down for some breakfast. Taking my clothes and the armament into the bathroom with me, I left the room door open for the room-service waiter. When I came out of the bathroom, shaved, showered, and dressed, the breakfast was waiting for me on a table near the open window. I divided myself between Greek orange juice, Greek honey, and the Greek view. All three of them were all right; and then suddenly, because one of them went wrong, none of them were any good to me any more.

It was the view that soured it. There was a stretch of the world's bluest water rimmed by a ribbon of the world's whitest beach. Behind the beach rose a rugged line of hills, and the hillsides were pocketed with more little terraced places than a man could count. Any place a farmer could find a toehold he'd climbed up and planted something just so it could burst into bloom that morning for Matthew Erridge to look at with his breakfast. Against this terraced backdrop sat the town. It was white and gleaming. Some kid had put it together out of hundreds and hundreds of neat rectangular pieces of the best lump sugar. Some of the sugar lumps had flags flying from the top of them, and the flags had been made for the town. They were as blue as the sea, and as white as the beach.

There was the boat landing and the place alongside it where we'd left the car the night before. The place was empty. There were other cars parked in the area, but not the heap Mom had been stuck with by the car-hire people. I looked hard at every car in sight, and there wasn't one even of the same make. It had vanished.

I had binoculars in my bag, and with them I brought every car parked along that waterfront right up into my lap. I saw at least a dozen cars that maybe were worth swiping, but that worthless crate was gone.

I checked my pocket and brought out the key, I hadn't left it in the car. I hadn't left it with Jake and Roy. I hadn't given it to Mom. I had it.

So any fool who's even a little handy with wires can jump the ignition and drive the car away. I wasn't impressed with the way the Greek fuzz handled murder, but the time had come for trying them out on something a little easier, like car theft. Dropping the car key back in my pocket, I left my breakfast. As I came out of my room, I was pressing my arm tight against my side. I liked the feel of the little pistol between my arm and ribs.

I thought I'd have a word with Mom before I went ashore and looked for the fuzzorium. I also thought Grymm might want to come with me in case of language problems. Both their doors stood open, and chambermaids were busy in both rooms. I went through, thinking the gals might be out on their balconies, but they weren't.

Down in the garden? Looking over the railings, I could see a swimming pool down there and umbrella-shaded tables around it. I rode the elevator down. In the corridor between the two massive doors was a desk. An English-speaking clerk was on duty. I asked him if he had seen either of the ladies.

He had seen both of them. Both had been down very early. Mrs. Grymm had gone ashore just before sunup. He remarked that it had been very early for going ashore, hours before any of the shops would be open, too early for anything but going out with the fishermen, which was probably what she had done. The Americans and the English seemed to like doing that, even the ladies. I could see it was a taste that was never going to turn him on, but this was a live-and-let-live cat.

"And where's Mrs. Erridge gone?" I asked.

"Mrs. Erridge," he purred, indicating that Mom was something else again. Mom was the kind of guest they wanted in this de luxe hangman's rest. She'd never let them down by tangling herself up with common people and fishnets. "Mrs. Erridge is off on a day's yachting," he said.

It had to be the old trouble, hotel English, all sound and no meaning.

"A day's yachting? In a boat? On the water?"

He had a moment's impulse to tell me to go away and stop bothering him, but he'd been handed a status symbol. He wasn't throwing it away.

"We've had all the great yachts putting in here, sir," he said. "We are much favored by yachtsmen."

I didn't need quotes from the brochure. "Whose yacht?" I asked.

He told me they got all of them. He rattled off a list—Prince Whichovitch, Count Whosi, the Duke of Things, the Earl of Stuff, the Baron of Nonsense.

"Mrs. Erridge?" I tried again. "She's on whose yacht?"

"Friends of her son."

"Name?"

"I didn't get a name," he said loftily. "When no name is mentioned, one assumes it's an incognito. One respects it."

I want to think this is the original kook out of Cloudcuckooland. Why not? It was a Greek who invented it, Aristophanes; but where was Mom?

"Could we," I said, "take this all the way back to the first chorus and run it through again, slowly and softly?"

Obviously we can't. "May I suggest, sir," he murmurs, "begging your pardon, sir, may I suggest that where Mrs. Erridge and her son go, what they do, and with whom, is neither your affair nor mine?"

"You can suggest it," I murmur back at him, "but not to me because I'm Mrs. Erridge's son, and I haven't a friend in the world."

He laughs, but only because it's polite to laugh at a man's jokes, and what I've said has got to be a joke even if he doesn't dig it. It's the American sense of humor, peculiar.

"You can't be."

"Who says I can't?"

"Because Mr. Erridge isn't here. He's with his mother."

I fetch up my passport and flip it across the desk. He picks it up and looks at it. He looks at the picture, and he looks at me. He scrambles among the registration cards and comes up with mine. He compares card and passport. He gulps.

"You have a brother?" he says.

He's not so much asking me if I have one. He's begging me to have one. I'm not unsympathetic. If Erridge ever wanted a male sibling, he wants one now; but facts are facts, and they have to be faced.

"I am her only son," I say, slamming all doors on wishful thinking. "I have no brother."

He couldn't understand it. There had to be some most peculiar mistake. He'd taken the message himself, and he had relayed it to Mom. Not very long after Mrs. Grymm had taken off, a most elegant motor launch had come slicing up to Hangman's Rest. A most superior sort of boatman had tied this most superior sort of craft up to the landing and had come to the desk. The clerk tended to linger over the elegance of the launch, and the impeccable speech, dress, and manners of the boatman. Since he was attached to a hotel much favored by all the best yachts, the clerk knew at sight the difference between the tender that served one of the great ones and any ordinary sort of launch-for-rent job. He also had the keenest perceptions of the difference between a seagoing flunky employed by one of the great ones and any ordinary waterfront character.

This top-drawer mariner had gone to the desk; and, in a manner so toploftily elegant that the clerk was obviously still switched on from having been subjected to it, asked the clerk to call Mrs. Erridge's room. With her son's most respectful compliments he was to tell Mrs. Erridge that Mr. Erridge had by the happiest of coincidences happened on some very old and very dear friends who by that happiest of coincidences happened to be yachting in these beautiful waters.

Mr. Erridge had joined his friends on their yacht, and the yacht's boatmen was even now below awaiting Mrs. Erridge's pleasure. Her son's friends were most eager to meet her. Her son was most eager that she meet his friends. Would she just as quickly as she could come down and join them aboard the yacht? If she hadn't already breakfasted, she wasn't to stop for that since nothing would give her son and her son's dear, dear friends greater delight than to have her grace their breakfast table.

"You gave her this message?"

"Yes, sir, I did."

"What did she say?"

"She was disturbed about going off and leaving the other lady;

but I was able to tell her Mrs. Grymm had already set off on an expedition of her own. She said she would be down in ten minutes. She was down in exactly nine, but since she used one minute to leave with me a message for Mrs. Grymm, it was precisely ten minutes the boatman waited for her."

You can dig how this cat was keeping his mind off the worrying main event by letting it dwell on Mom's admirable promptness and graciousness and the faultlessly upper-bracket appearance and manners of her kidnaper.

"What was the message she left Mrs. Grymm?" I asked.

"Only that you—that her son had happened on some friends and that she was going to join her son aboard their yacht. I was to tell Mrs. Grymm that, as soon as Mrs. Erridge knew what the program was to be, she would be in touch with Mrs. Grymm."

"But she hasn't been in touch?"

"Not yet. There's been no further word from her, sir; but Mrs. Grymm hasn't returned yet either. When they go out with the fishermen, you know, it's usually midafternoon before they're back."

He told me what the boatman looked like—a young Greek, superbly handsome with the superb build of a great athlete, well-spoken, well-bred. Maybe he was describing a man he'd seen, and maybe he was doing me a rough translation of one of those odes Pindar wrote to some fifth century B.C. paragon who brought an Olympic championship home to Athens. Either way he was drawing a picture that rang no bells for me.

"Was he alone? Nobody on the launch with him? Like some Arabs maybe?"

"Arabs? Oh, no, sir. There was a gentleman. I would say a Greek gentleman. He stayed below in the cabin, and the cabin door was shut. I saw the gentleman briefly. He opened the cabin door to ask the boatman if the message had been delivered, and if Mrs. Erridge was coming down. When the boatman told him ten minutes, he went back into the cabin and shut the door behind him. When the launch pulled away with Mrs. Erridge, he was still in the cabin with the door shut."

"Carefully not showing himself," I groaned. "Describe the man."

He did. The size of the lug, the heft, the streaks of silver in his black hair. It was an excellent description, fully detailed. It was like nobody Pindar ever wrote an ode to.

"Carries amber-colored worry beads with a green tassel?"

It made the clerk a lot happier verifying that detail for me. He'd begun being afraid that the men who had taken Mom away weren't friends of mine after all.

"Yes," he said. "I most particularly noticed his worry beads. Even a man like that, with all he has, needs them."

Philosophizing I didn't need. "How long have they been gone?" I asked.

He glanced at his watch. "Four, five hours."

I checked my own watch. It was still climbing up on nine. Even allowing for differences in the Greek Orthodox calendar, this wasn't April Fools' Day. What other day does any cat in his right mind try to tell a man that his mother, wakened by that message at four or five in the morning, graciously accepted the invitation, took no more than nine minutes to jump into her pants, and went gaily off for an early breakfast somewhere out on the briny.

"Four in the morning?" I barked. "Five in the morning?"

"No, sir. Four or five hours ago. It was just about eight o'clock. It's now twenty of one."

"My watch says twenty of nine," Erridge insisted, laying the eternal verities on the line, but even as he's saying it, he knows better. A cat has to make his choice of verities. The Rolex or the sun standing directly overhead. The thing's self-winding, shockproof, just-about-everything-elseproof, also infallible. So it was another thing to think about along with how late I slept.

Despite prevailing opinion to the contrary, I knew what had been done to me in Athens. But here in another hotel? In this impregnable fastness of a hotel? Who slipped Erridge a mickey here?

The why of it seemed clear enough. You have a plan afoot for the kidnaping of a cat's mother. You take steps to eliminate any opposition he might offer. I could think about the big effort made to prevent my finding Mom at the QP, but then I also had to think about the other big effort that in face of everything, including Erridge himself, did deliver me to Mom at the QP.

Okay. Call it two teams working toward opposite goals. So which is which? Who belongs on what team? How did they know I'd be coming by way of Cairo? Where did the Lily of Luxor fit into the picture? And my son of the desert turning up in Athens, not to speak of Arabs riding in convoy with us because they were scared of bandits?

The last thing I wanted to do was sit down and think this thing out. I wanted to jump in a boat and take off rapidly in all directions. I wanted to hit out. I could feel that little gun hugged up against my rib cage, and I wanted to use it. So, on what? Where do I go to find my target? Even if I can find it, how do I know it's my target? Two teams working toward opposite goals? Suppose I do get a chance at somebody. Suppose I do start shooting. Suppose I mow down Mom's team.

What could I do but sit and wait? I had the clerk phone Athens for me. He got me my man at the embassy, and he got me that top fuzz I'd had the go-around with the day before. They had news for me, the lab analysis of the whiskey glass. The glass was clean, not a trace of drugs.

"So you see, Mr. Erridge."

So those babies at the QP had the whole of that night for popping in and out of my room and washing glasses. Also I had news for them. It had happened again. Was it maybe a regular part of the service in all hotels in Greece?

They not only suggested that I was obsessive. They even took my English apart. A man, speaking correctly, can hardly be drugged again if he hasn't been drugged in the first place. I let that lay because I had more important news for them. Mom had been kidnaped, and I had at my side a hotel clerk who wasn't obsessive and who didn't have a lurid imagination. I would put this man on, and in his own words he would describe to them Mom's abductor and the circumstances of her abduction. I would leave it to them to determine whether his description did or did not tally with my description of the herculean lug who had given me a hard time at the Axilles way back there when I first landed in Athens.

Both embassy and fuzz listened. Both assured me that everything possible would be done. I was to sit tight and wait to hear from them. Both finished by asking me the same question. Was I certain that I'd told them everything? Was there not something that I might have forgotten; or, if I would forgive their suggesting it, chosen not to reveal to them?

Bitterness took over. I told them the problem wasn't my not telling them everything. It was their not believing enough of what I told them. Then with the cops I did embarrassingly remember that there was more. I'd been letting it slip away from me.

I had to back up and complete the package: the cars that trailed us into Corinth and then picked us up again after Corinth for the rest of the ride, my seeing Leonidas and the nut salesman just as we were pulling away from the QP, our picking up Roy and Jake in Corinth, the disappearance of the hired car even though I still had the ignition key in my pocket, the appearance of the Sonof at the cafe across from the QP, the report I'd had from Roy and Jake that at least part of the pursuit had been Arabs, probably the bodyguard of my Sonof.

I'd seen Leonidas, and I hadn't called a cop. Hearing that turned them on, but big. Why hadn't I called a cop? I'd led them to believe I was going to cooperate better than that. Also now that I'd brought to mind this supreme piece of folly, picking up hitchhikers—a practice frowned on by fuzz the world over— would I please cudgel the old head some more and see whether I hadn't committed some other sin of imbecility and let it slip my mind. If I was going to go around the country picking up hitchhikers, how could I possibly expect that I wouldn't have my car stolen?

They'd been thinking I had better sense, but now that they knew I had no sense at all, everything they'd told me before went double. I was to sit tight at my beautiful island hotel. I'd be hearing from them.

I did nothing, but I couldn't sit tight. I swarmed all over the ramparts of my island prison. From every vantage point I searched for yachts, looking for motor launches, fishing boats, anything that floated. Each boat I picked up I hoped would be it. Each one I studied through the glasses.

I didn't expect to spot Mom sporting about on the decks of one of these craft. All I was asking for was a glimpse of someone I'd recognize—Kostya Leonidas, Heracles, the Sonof, any of his bodyguards, Roy and/or Jake.

In every direction I was drawing blanks. Then a boy came up to call me to the phone. I took the call in my room. It had a window that commanded at least a section of the watery panorama. It wasn't the fuzz. It was the embassy. They'd heard from the police, and they were burning up the wires. For what? To give Erridge a lecture. No. Two lectures.

No. 1: As a nation we take a dim view of individual citizens who meddle in the internal affairs of other nations. Assistance given by an engineer to the development of an underdeveloped country was much approved of. Meddling in the internal politics of said underdeveloped country was frowned upon. Taking a violent hand in such politics was simply never done. It was within the power of the Department of State to see that it wasn't done. They can lift a cat's passport any time they think it advisable.

I explained as patiently as I could that, if this was a matter that in any way involved the internal politics of an underdeveloped nation, they had better climb down off Erridge's back and suggest to my underdeveloped Sonof that he quit letting his underdeveloped internal politics meddle with me or with my mom.

"Just a word of warning, Mr. Erridge."

"Up yours," Erridge snarled.

No. 2: Impoverished, young American males, hitchhiking around Greece. This was a matter of great concern to all Americans, and we must all cooperate in a concerted effort to discourage these shameless youths and make their shameful racket unworkable. They were swarming into the country and converging on Mount Athos. The word had gotten around. Only a hundred drachmas, roughly three bucks, bought a man a permit to visit the monastery area.

After that it was the traditional hospitality of the monks. That initial three bananas paid for what was amounting to a license for freeloading at the monasteries for any indefinite period. Those Mount Athos monks carried Christian charity to excess. They provided food, drink, and shelter. No questions asked. They required nothing in return, not even good behavior. Although they did deplore hell-raising, their charity covered even that. The thinner-skinned of these freeloading cats did move from monastery to monastery, but even so they were putting an uncarriable load on the monasteries' resources. Some of them, furthermore, were so crude about it that they found a monastery that suited them and simply settled in.

The car, I was assured, would be recovered. The fuzz would be watching for it along the roads going north. Roy and Jake would be picked up when they headed into the Mount Athos peninsula, if not sooner; but meanwhile, by giving the two boys a lift, Erridge had made his contribution to an international scandal.

"They thumbed me going south," I protested. "From Corinth down to here. It's the wrong way for Mount Athos."

So the boys had taken a small detour. For a chance to swipe a car, that little extra mileage was worth it.

So it was back to the ramparts and again scanning the waters for the kidnap craft. I got to feeling like one of those old New England dames watching from her widow's walk for her man's sail to come up over the horizon. It did seem as though there should have been something more useful for me to do, but what? Dip some candles? Hook a rug? Quilt a coverlet?

The afternoon went on forever. If the astronomers think the earth rotates at an even pace, I have news for them. That day *it* knocked off and left the sun hanging up there in that one spot just past the zenith for a flock of eternities.

Then suddenly it pulled up its socks and started whirling around like crazy. The day that was never going to end began rushing toward night. The sun couldn't be closing on the horizon that fast unless its parachute had failed to open. Erridge went into a panic. It was going to be only a matter of minutes before the dark would be closing in, and he was going to have to give up even this fruitless watching.

Then in just those closing minutes of daylight a cabin cruiser came scudding into the channel between my island and the mainland. It had more flash to it than anything I'd seen all afternoon, and it was sleek enough, luxurious enough, and elegant enough to have impressed hell out of that desk clerk.

It gave off a lot of glitter, and I quickly recognized that not all of it was bouncing off the polished brass. Some of it was reflection of the setting sun sent my way by the lenses in a row of binoculars. If I was interested in the cruiser, the cruiser was interested in me. Through my own glasses I could pick them out. It was three pair of binoculars in a row. It was also three familiar figures in a row, my son of the desert, flanked by two of his bodyguards. For a moment I thought they were coming to the island, but they headed for the mainland instead. They pulled in alongside the boat landing, that same one where we had embarked for the executioners' pad, the one where I left the car.

The boat tied up, but nobody left it. The three of them just sat there, watching me through their glasses. It was too much. I'd been told to stay put. I'd been told to leave everything to the fuzz. I'd been told to keep my cottonpickin' fingers out of stuff I didn't understand. I'd been told and told and told, but the whole afternoon had gone by, and nobody had produced Mom or even any news of her.

Hugging my arm against my side because I liked the feel of the little pistol against my ribs, I nipped downstairs. The hotel boatman had just cast off; but, pausing only long enough for a glance toward shore to check on whether they were still there and still watching, I took a flying jump for the boat and made it.

I was hoping the boatman might understand English or Italian or something I could handle. If that cruiser made a move, we were going to take off after it, even if I had to tranquilize the boatman with Leonidas's worry beads and run the boat myself.

The problem didn't arise. The cabin cruiser stayed put. The bodyguards did go into action; and although I watched their every move as we drew up on them, I could see nothing that looked hostile. They were bringing out bottles and glasses. They brought up a big, round tin, set in a bowl of ice; and I knew what that was—caviar. The Sonof was too Moslem to be anything but teetotal, but in his book nothing went with Coke like caviar. I'd been through this before. For Erridge there would be champagne. Sure enough. The last ray the sun threw that evening glanced off the polished silver sides of the champagne bucket.

It was the cocktail hour, was it not? Erridge was coming aboard, was he not? Move it anywhere you like, desert hospitality is still desert hospitality. I didn't wait for my boat to come around into the landing. We came alongside the cabin cruiser on our way in, and I jumped for it. It wasn't the caviar that was pulling me, and it wasn't the champagne. It wasn't even the Coke.

"Mr. Erridge," said the Sonof. "This is a coincidence."

"Is it?" I snarled. I wasn't calling him "your highness."

"You're in bad temper, my boy," he said, all silk and sympathy. "You're not having a good holiday?"

"I'm not."

"A drink will make you feel better. Champagne, or do you prefer your whiskey?" He waved toward a bottle. Since he was watching me closely, he must have seen me blink. It was my brand. "You didn't think I knew the kind you favor," he said. "There is nothing that escapes my attention, Mr. Erridge, nothing ever."

With anyone else you might call it horsing about. With these sons of the desert, it's the way they do business. Never say anything you can talk around. I wasn't playing it his way.

"You're not back home," I told him. "Back there it's maybe called the royal will. Here it's kidnaping."

I thought I was past being surprised by anything, but he surprised me. The one thing I expected he'd like the least was plain speaking. He liked it fine, even the word "kidnaping."

"You are in no position to complain, Mr. Erridge," he purred. "At home I would have called it the man succumbing to the natural hazards of his job and his incompetence. Here they call it murder."

I wasn't holding still for any change of subject. "I want her," I said, "and I want her now."

I was closing in on him, and out of the corners of my eyes I saw the bodyguards move along with me; but, before they got on me, he made what looked like a mistake. He waved them off, and he let me come in close. I had my hand slipped inside my shirt; but the way it looked, I was just scratching. A man scratching is never anything that'll worry them. Where they come from it's one of the universal acts, like breathing or like circulating blood. Everybody is doing it, and all the time.

As soon as I was between him and them, I brought my hand out and with it the little gun. I had a good grip on it, and I had my trigger finger slipped through the trigger guard. Picking just the right spot in the tallow he carried above the waistband of his pants, I rammed the muzzle in hard. Just then the hotel boatman came whizzing past with a covey of new guests for the executioners' pad. We rocked gently in his wake.

With the rocking, the trigger of my little pistol swung back and forth against my finger. It hit my finger and swung away, hit and swung away. There was no tension to it. Somewhere, sometime, somehow, someone had stripped the little thing down, removed its trigger spring, and put it back together again as good as new except for the one important difference. A trigger when it's hanging loose is just about as functional as the tassel on a string of worry beads.

It had been all right in the gunshop. I had tested it. Nobody ever misses checking out the tension of the trigger spring. From weapon to weapon there'll always be some shade of difference there, and it's a difference that can mean that, when you want to squeeze your shot off, you might be a fraction of a second too soon with it or a fraction of a second too late.

I wanted desperately to take that gun out of his gut and have a good look at it, but I'd made my move and I was stuck with it. I held steady, digging the weapon a little deeper into him.

He held steady, too. He was never a coward. He couldn't be, not the way fraternal feeling ran in his family.

"You'll trust me to take you to her?" he said.

"I'll trust you," I told him.

He was reading me loud and clear. As long as I had a gun on him, I'd trust him. I had to hope, of course, that he wasn't reading the rest of me, that he didn't know I was even less dangerous than a kid with a cap pistol. The kid, at least, can make a loud noise. I couldn't make anything.

"Back in the hills," he said.

"We go by car?"

"Yes. It's too far to walk."

"Okay. Tell the bodyguards to stay here. We'll go alone, you and I. You'll drive, and I'll keep you honest."

"Impossible," he said, and he turned a little white.

I dug in a little harder with the gun muzzle. "Necessity," I said, "is invention's mom."

"You'll defeat both of us," he said. "I never have dismissed them that way. They'll know something is very wrong, and they'll act on their own. You know what that'll mean."

"For you a bullet in the belly."

"And for you, Mr. Erridge, their knives in your back, an outcome neither to your advantage or to mine."

I had to do it his way. They brought the inevitable Cadillac around, and we headed for the hills. Going ashore and getting into the car, I had to palm the gun and step away from the Sonof for a bit, but he played along. One bodyguard took the wheel and the other sat in the other front seat. My Sonof and I were alone in back. I picked a lower spot, where shooting him would be meaner, and so kept the gun out of range of the rear-vision mirror.

He held still for it, and that bugged me. Did I have him that convinced that I was ready and able to squeeze one off? Or did he know that with every lurch of the car that swinging trigger was bobbing back and forth and tickling my finger?

We went back the way we'd come in the night before. I recognized the spot where we'd lost our tail. I was guessing that they were taking me to wherever it was the Cadillacs had gone the night before; and I wanted to make myself believe it would be where they were holding Mom. What had me bugged was how they got her there. The clerk's account of how she was tricked into the boat was reasonable enough. She could have been snowed by that, but then how did they persuade her to go ashore, climb into a car, and go off with them into the hills? What kind of a yacht climbs mountains? Had they drugged her? Slugged her? What had they done to her?

At the crest of the hill behind the town we turned off the road into a tree-shaded driveway. They were double-purpose trees, providing concealment as well as shade. Anything could happen inside that place; and, whatever the traffic along the road, nothing would be seen and nothing heard.

The driveway dipped down into a hollow, and then it climbed again. At the top of the rise we drew up before a large villa. It was pink with lavender trim, vaguely Hispano-Moresque. It was Hollywood of the 1920 vintage. It had a band of broad windows across its front. They were the wrong size and the wrong shape for the kind of house it was, but they commanded a panoramic view of the waterfront, the sea, and of the little island where once the aging executioners dozed away their declining years.

The Cadillac parked alongside the house. I caught myself thinking this was nice for the Cadillac, coming up here where it could be among friends. There were three others just like it parked up there, and in among them stood the hired heap for which the Greek fuzz had set up a watch on every road leading toward Mount Athos.

We left the car as we entered it. I palmed the pistol, but again the Sonof took no advantage of the awkward moment. Once we were out of the car, he worked at making it even easier for me. He told the bodyguards to stay outside with the Cadillacs, and he led me into the house.

Inside it was like I'd never gone away. They were all there, six of the brothers, and you could think they didn't even know they weren't back at the rear gate to nowhere. The four, who always played bridge, were playing bridge. The two, who were always reading, had their books, and even the books were the same. One had gone to school in England, the other in France. The English-educated one was reading *Fanny Hill.* The French-educated one was reading Baudelaire. They were all drinking coffee.

The Sonof looked at them, and he looked at me. He had been expecting something from this confrontation. I didn't know what, and I cared less. I flipped the pistol out of my palm, and I leveled it at him.

"This," I said, "is your family reunion. I want mine."

The brothers looked at the pistol. The six of them might have been dancing from the one puppet-string, and somebody pulled it. Coming at me from every side, they took me. My finger tightened on the trigger, but it was only a reflex. If I'd had a working trigger on that pistol, the Sonof would have been a dead potentate, and the brothers would have had the back gate to nowhere up for grabs.

They let me up and they handed the pistol to the Sonof. He had the shakes so bad that the little gun was jumping in his hand, and you could hear the tinkle of the trigger as it swung free inside the trigger guard. Pulling himself together, he snarled at the brothers. They went back to their reading and their bridge game. Then he turned to me.

"You must learn whom you can trust," he said.

"I trust nobody."

"You think they were trying to save me?"

"I'm not thinking about them or about you."

He told me it was time I started thinking. He recommended that I think about the way they jumped me, carefully giving me all the time I needed to squeeze off my shot.

"You thought you knew what you were to do for them."

It was a picture I could draw for myself. When they'd jumped me, it had, of course, been because they'd seen a chance of getting the Sonof killed, and they'd been quick to take it. I'd take the rap for murder. They'd have him out of the way.

"Where is she?" I said.

"There are more important questions, Mr. Erridge."

"Not to me, there aren't."

"To me. I'll show you something."

He started from the room, beckoning me to follow him. I didn't need the invitation. I was still with it. I was even glad to be rid of that silly pistol. Given another chance, I still had Leonidas's worry beads and my own two mitts. He, however, had his pair of bodyguards back on station.

We went down a narrow hall and at the end of it down a flight of narrow stairs. At the bottom of the stairs he kicked a door open. We went into a cellar room. It had no windows, only the door we came in by and another at the far end. The far door led out of the building. I had been adding up distances all the way, and this was as far as the villa extended.

The room was unfurnished except for a couple of heavy wooden chairs. On one of the chairs lay a small heap of rags and slung across the rags a pair of light, braided whips. In the middle of the room were Jake and Roy. They had been stripped naked. They were tied by the wrists to an overhead beam, and it was lucky for them that they had so much size to them and that this cellar had a relatively low ceiling. In another room, big as they were, their feet would have been off the floor. They would have been hanging. Here they weren't quite that bad off. Their feet were taking some of their weight.

Knobbly, purplish welts crisscrossed their backs. Those whips had been laid on across their shoulders, but otherwise they were unmarked. They'd been put through the first stage of the treatment, but they'd been made ready for what would be coming next.

The Sonof was expecting me to be impressed. I had only the one question.

"Where is she?"

This time he answered me. Hadn't I seen her on the way in? Also what was so important about her? She'd never been much of a car. He was disappointed in me. He was coming to think I'd never understood him. He was a man who rewarded his friends and punished his enemies. His rewards were as lavish as his punishments. All he'd ever asked of me was that I do my job, and I could have had any sort of car I wanted, if that was what I wanted. He'd never asked me for any help in dealing with his brothers, but he hadn't expected that I would throw in with them either.

I tried to straighten him around. It wasn't the car I'd been looking for. It was Mom. I wasn't interested in him or his brothers. I wanted Mom, and I wanted her intact and untouched. It was obvious that he had never understood me. In the rewards department I didn't pretend to compete, but I could also be lavish, and I meant in the punishments department.

So now I was asking again. "Where is she?"

He didn't know, but he knew how to find out. His brothers would know, and he was ready to make a deal. If I gave him what he wanted, he would get it out of his brothers. It would be no problem.

"You made your mistake when you trusted them," he said. "If she's been taken, it's they who've taken her. She's their guarantee that you'll do for them what you undertook to do."

"I undertook nothing, no more for them than for you."

"Why did you come here?"

"To have a holiday. To see my mother."

"Why did you kill Hamid?"

"The Lily of Luxor? I didn't kill him."

"He's of no importance, except for one thing. What did he find out about you? What made him worth killing?"

"If you don't know, ask your brothers. It's you or them. I never had any part of it."

He indicated Roy and Jake. "They could have talked," he said. "They never would have been hurt at all."

"Maybe they have nothing to talk about," I suggested. "Maybe they know no more about what's going on than I do."

He said he knew more than I thought he did. The brothers had all gone abroad, one by one, each to a different innocent destination; but his agents—Hamid had been one and Constantine Leonidas was another—had reported that from all the various places they had gone the brothers were converging on Greece. They had taken this villa in the hills. They were converging here.

Then, he told me, I made my first mistake. I telephoned Athens. He had a report on the call. It seemed innocent enough, but he knew better. Athens wasn't innocent. It was too close to where the brothers were. Then I took off, but I would be easy. It was a flakily simple-minded conspirator who'd run a phone call through the Sonof's switchboard. He counted on me to give the whole show away.

Even a half-competent spy like Hamid could go through my bag and find something useful. I'd have something written down. If it wasn't in my bag, it would be on my person. Hamid picked up my bag. Hamid followed me to the hotel; and, while I was in the bathroom, he picked up my pants. Hamid found nothing which had to mean Hamid had muffed it. The Sonof's man in Cairo laid into Hamid. That's how the Lily of Luxor got the cut hand, but Hamid begged for a second chance. They flew him out to Athens to wait for me there.

Leonidas, however, was to get the first Athens play. He was to try a friendly approach. If that failed, Hamid would have his second chance. So Leonidas made no time with me, and Hamid was trying again. That time Hamid came up dead, sufficient proof that Erridge had thrown in with the brothers.

But the proof kept piling up. Hamid was dead, and Leonidas had to get out of the hotel. Who but our old buddy, Matthew Erridge, turned up in the basement to try to stop him? And then what? Erridge leaves Athens, and where does he go?

The brothers were assembled and ready to make their play, whatever it might be. All of the Sonof's cohorts had to be gathered in and brought to this villa where the brothers were. Nobody can be left in Athens to keep an eye on Erridge. So then what happens? Constantine Leonidas spots the hired heap parked by the boat landing. Erridge is in town, too, and Erridge has his men keeping watch by his car.

The Sonof moves in and takes over at the villa. He picks up Roy and Jake, and he's waiting for them to start talking. Now Erridge walks into his hands. So the time has come for Erridge to smarten up. His whole enterprise is down the hole. If he takes a good look at his friends, he will come to his senses. All he has to do is talk now, and he can spare himself a lot of grief. He's going to talk sooner or later.

"Questions," I say. "Who pulled the trigger spring out of my gun? Who drugged me last night and the night before?"

If I wanted the answers, I could have them by talking. Once I talked, he'd get the rest of it out of the brothers.

I was adding it up differently. I was about to tell him he couldn't have it both ways. The brothers wreck my pistol, and then they count on me with that same pistol to dispose of the Sonof.

I'm starting on telling him that, but he isn't listening. He pulls out of the cellar and leaves me to the bodyguards. They come at me from all sides and pin me down. They drag me to the empty chair. Slamming me down into it, they tie me down. My legs are lashed tight to the heavy chair legs. A rope goes around my chest and the back of the chair, another across my thighs and under the chair seat. I am tied wrist and elbow to the chair arms.

When I've been well secured, they pick me up, chair and all, and position me carefully. They put me where I have the best view of those welts that crisscross the backs of the two boys. Then they leave me.

X

"He's not kidding, Matt," Jake spoke up.

"He didn't tell you," Roy added. "He's got Mrs. Grymm, too."

While I was fruitlessly testing my ropes, they fed me what the Sonof hadn't. They'd been awake and taking an early swim when they saw Mrs. Grymm come ashore. Four men they recognized closed around her as soon as she stepped ashore. They were the men who had followed me into Corinth and shown so much interest in the car while I was inside having coffee. The kids explained why they hadn't pitched right in to help her.

They'd been in the water barebutt with their clothes up on the beach. Not knowing how Grymm would take it if they came out of the water that way, they'd hesitated. By the time their nakedness began seeming a minor matter, they were too late. The four characters had gone off with Grymm in a waiting Cadillac.

The kids swam for the beach, and all the time they watched the retreating lights of the Cadillac. They would see the lights and then lose them around a curve, and then they would come back into view again. The Cadillac was climbing the hill road, all the way to the crest. They were skinning into their clothes when they saw the lights stop at the big villa on top.

They figured going out to the island to tell me about it would lose time, and all they could be saving themselves might be a little embarrassment. If it was all right, and I would tell them so, then there'd be no harm in going up to the villa without talking to me. It might annoy Grymm, but she didn't like them anyhow.

If, on the other hand, it was the way it looked, they would better be moving. They jumped the ignition on the heap and took off. At the crest they came to the villa. They had no doubt of its being the right one. The covey of Cadillacs was parked outside.

I'd given up on the ropes. I was working the only way I could. By digging my feet hard against the floor, I could move the chair slightly. I had to put every last ounce of strength into it, but I was scraping it along, a fraction of an inch at a time. I paused to let some of the sweat roll off me.

"Including the car they took Grymm in?" I asked.

"They all look the same," Jake said. "All we knew was here's where the Cadillacs go."

I saved my breath for scraping my chair along, shifting it painfully and slowly toward Jake. He's nearer, and I have to get there before they come back.

Except for the Cadillacs, the boys could see no sign of life at the villa. The place was all buttoned up. They ranged around the house looking for a chink in the shutters. Before they'd tried even half the shutters, they were jumped from behind and dragged into the house.

"They didn't start flogging on us right off," Roy said.

"At first it was like social," Jake explained.

They were taken to the Sonof, and he had them brought along to where the brothers were assembled.

"It was like your friend expected us to show we recognized somebody. Four cats playing bridge and two boning up on sex. Us to recognize them or them us."

"Did you?"

"No."

"What about the four who took Grymm?"

"They haven't shown," Jake said.

"Maybe they're working on her," Roy muttered.

I dropped the questions, and again I put all my strength into scraping that chair along.

"You're coming closer," Jake said. "We did that, too."

"What?"

"Moved the chairs."

It was the way the treatment began, they explained. When they insisted they knew nothing, they'd been tied into the chairs and left alone. They'd discovered they could edge the chairs along, and they were given all the time they needed for it.

"It was to show us we couldn't do ourselves any good except we talked," Roy said. "We got our chairs right together and we tried to get so we could work on each other's knots, but it's no go. If you're tied the way we were, you can't get your fingers up far enough off the chair arm to get at anything."

"The way we were," Jake put in, "we could just not reach each other's knots. We were missing by maybe an inch."

"They'll give you time enough to get to us and to wear yourself out trying to do something about it when you get here, and then . . ."

That was good news. I knew this about the Sonof. He had a set routine for everything he did, and he always followed his routines. It looked like he was going to give me all the time I needed. With that encouragement, I found some extra strength I never knew I had. I came up behind Jake.

"Okay," I said. "You try to jackknife up so you can get your feet on my knees. I'll keep pushing in under you."

He dug it right off, except that Erridge was asking the impossible. Jake would have to bring his legs up while he let the whole of his weight hang from the rope that tied his wrists. Maybe it's a trick a cat can do if he's had the time to practice it enough, but he can spend his whole life working out in a gym and never think of preparing himself for that one.

Maybe you think it's nothing much, the simplest routine of trapeze work, but there's all the difference in the world between what you can do if you're hanging by your hands and what you can do when you're hanging from a rope that's tied around your wrists. Also there's a difference between what you can do when you first hang up there and what after you've been hanging a while.

He kept trying, and all the time I was expecting he'd quit and tell me it was the same as before. The Sonof knew we would try this, and he was giving us all the time we needed to learn just how helpless we were. Maybe he was thinking it, but he was saying nothing. He was giving it everything he had.

So was I. I kept edging in, bit by bit, pushing his feet out from under him, giving him something to lay his weight against. He gave up struggling, but I wasn't worrying any. I knew what he was doing. He was waiting for the moment when I would have come far enough, so that he could climb up my legs. He was gathering his strength for it.

It was forever. When I looked up, the welts that ridged his back were coming so close to my eyes that I was seeing them double. I had to force myself to concentrate on moving the chair. Again and again I caught myself straining against the ropes. I was so close. It seemed impossible that I couldn't just reach out and lift him.

My knees came in under his knees, and scrape by scrape I pushed on them, making them bend. Slowly I was raising him up, lifting his feet off the ground, folding him into my lap. I wasn't raising him up much, but it was enough. The whole of his weight came to rest on me. The pull came off the rope around his wrists. I felt him tense as he put every muscle into it, and he hooked his fingers over the top of the beam. That gave him the purchase he needed. He brought his legs up, and he was standing on my knees.

Now that his weight was off it, there was enough play in the rope between his wrists, so that he could get his fingers around to cope with the knots, but he had to have some blood back into those fingers before he could make them do anything at all. His numbed hands were just slipping off the knots.

"Take your time, kid," Roy groaned. "Rub your hands a while first. Get some feeling back into them. You'll make it."

"While you're still hanging?" Jake came back at him. "How comfortable do I make myself while you're still hanging?"

"Comfortable enough to do me some good, Charlie."

Jake rubbed his hands. I could feel the sweat pour off him. His hands were giving him all the hell of coming back to life. I knew he wasn't nearly ready when he started working on the knots again, but it was no good telling him to wait. He was a long time getting himself untied, but he made it and dropped to the floor. He started for Roy, and I didn't know how to tell him to quit. I didn't have to tell him. Roy did.

"Matt's next, Charlie," he said. "You want to keep your arms down for a while. Get Matt loose to do the overhead work."

He did my right hand first and then my right elbow. That freed me a hand to work on the rope around my chest. The knot on that one and the one that tied me to the seat were both in reach. It was one of their nice touches, putting them where I could see them and not get at them.

I couldn't do much one-handed, but I made a start; and when he had my left hand freed as well, I made short work of the rope around my chest. Jake got down to my ankles while I attacked the knot that held me down to the seat.

As soon as I was free, I pulled the chair over to where Roy was still hanging. I grabbed him around the knees and lifted, standing him on the chair. Even while I was clambering up beside him, he was already rubbing the blood back into his hands. He let me handle the job of getting him untied. I could do it faster, and he could use the time for bringing his hands back to life.

Jake meanwhile climbed into his clothes; and when we came down off the chair, he was standing by with Roy's stuff. I helped Roy pull on his few ragged threads. Jake picked up the two whips. He kept one for himself and handed the other to Roy. Roy looked at the thing blankly, but seeing the way Jake was holding his, he began to dig. Those whips had stubby weighted handles. Turn them wrong end to, and you have a neat little club.

"You got anything?" Roy asked me.

I wrapped Kostya's worry beads around my knuckles. "Brass knucks," I said. "Greek version."

We had a choice—back through the house or out the cellar door. The house was tempting but impossible. We knew the concentration of troops we were up against in that direction. The cellar door would take us out back of the house, into unknown territory. That the door would be unguarded was too much to ask, but I was riding on what I knew of the way the Sonof operated. He didn't have the troops for heavy concentrations everywhere. He liked having his men close around him, and the buckos he didn't keep directly attached to his precious person would always be assigned to watch over the transport. It's old desert custom. Guard the chief's person and the chief's camels. Back of the house he had to be spread thin.

I examined the cellar door, trying the knob cautiously. It turned without sound. I looked at the hinges. They were glistening with oil. I looked for the light switch, none in the room. It figured to be back inside, at the head of the cellar stairs. I climbed on one of the chairs and, using my shirttail to protect my hand, unscrewed light bulbs. Roy took one door and Jake the other, waiting to bop anything that came through. Nothing came.

I took the knob again in the dark. The kids flattened against the wall either side of the door. I waited while our eyes adjusted to the dark. Then I eased the door open. There was about ten feet of clear space back from the door. Beyond rose a dark array of lemon trees. I could smell them in the evening air. They were backed by a windbreak of taller trees. Those silhouetted clearly against the moon bathed evening sky. Just short of the lemon trees a glowing spark arced off in short flight and disappeared into the grass. It was too red for firefly glow, and it didn't have the firefly's dancing flight. It would be the burning butt of a cigarette carelessly flicked away.

Where you have a cigarette, you have a smoker. I strained against the dark of the lemon-tree shadows, trying to make him out. It wasn't all that hard. The white robe caught some of the moonglow. He was standing with his back to us. He wasn't watching for anything that would be coming at him from the villa. He was looking for something to steal up on him through the lemon trees.

He had something slung on his shoulder. I could see the dark line of the strap where it sliced across his back. The muzzle looked too thick for a rifle barrel. I guessed a shotgun. He lit another cigarette.

I looked off to either side of him. I could see nothing. If it was a picket line, the other sentries would be non-smokers. That wasn't likely. I stepped back for a brief conference.

"One man," I whispered. "He's watching the woods. He has his back to us. I'll go out alone and take him. I tangle him up, and you two take off. If I get it made, I'll come right after you. Don't wait to help me. Take off and come back with the fuzz. I'll be all right for that long."

"No," Roy growled.

"These two," Jake added, "don't run them out of whips."

"They've got Mom. We're wasting time."

I moved out. I wanted to look back and see if they were doing as I told them, but I couldn't take my eyes off the sentry. The footing couldn't have been better. It was a lawn that had been nursed along by some baby who loved grass. No dry leaves to rustle, no loose stones to rattle.

He carried the cigarette in his right hand. He brought it up to his mouth, dragged on it, and took it away again, all in a steady, unvarying rhythm. As I crept up on him, I was studying the timing. I wanted to be on him just as he brought the cigarette to his mouth, when his gun hand wouldn't be cocked for action. I wasn't afraid of getting shot. He'd never have the time to get it unlimbered and come around to point it at me. The idea was that he wasn't to have the time to get off any warning blast.

I was within five feet of him when he flicked the cigarette away and adjusted the gun on his shoulder. I crouched behind him and waited for his hands to come away from the gun. I was cursing myself for not having moved faster. Even the moment

I'd used up arguing with Jake and Roy would have made the difference. I cursed them a little, too. Then I stopped cursing, and I knew I was happy again because I could feel the big grin split my kisser. He was fumbling around in his robes. He was needing another cigarette, of course. With the flash of the match I moved in. He had both his hands tied up lighting the cigarette, and with the match flaring up in front of him he was seeing nothing out of the corners of his eyes.

I rammed my knee into the small of his back. My left hand grabbed his gun sling and pulled on it hard. Holding him steady for it, I chopped at his head with my right. Kostya's tranquilizers struck home. Match and cigarette fell into the grass, and he would have gone with them if I hadn't been holding him up, limp on his gun belt. Carefully I lowered him to that lovely lawn and unslung the gun from his shoulder. I'd been wrong. It was a tommygun.

I moved into the lemon trees carrying it at the ready. Easing my finger back against the trigger, I met the resistance. Nobody had been playing games with this baby. I would have loved to turn back and blast every window in that villa, to let the noise of my shooting bring the fuzz while I mowed down every man that showed. There was only one thing stopping me. "No good," I kept telling myself. "It's no good. Somewhere in there behind one of those windows, they've got Mom. It's not like I could think she's safe down in the cellar. I've been in the cellar."

Roy and Jake came up beside me. I should have thought to ask if they ever had infantry training. I gave the hand signals and hoped they'd dig me. They'd had the training. They split off to right and left; and, moving along even with me, they advanced into the woods.

We had come around behind this ridge the night before. I knew about these woods. They rode the crest; and, thick as they were, they didn't run deep. It was just the narrow band of them and then the ground would be dropping away to that road we had taken to skirt the rise and come down into the town.

There would be traffic on that road. I wasn't counting on anybody giving us a lift. Even in a country where they've never heard of bandits, you don't stop to pick up a cat who's using a tommygun to flag you down. There was going to be that passing car. The driver was going to see the tommygun. He was going to stamp his gas pedal down to the floorboards and run screaming into town to tell the fuzz about bandits in the hills. Up would come a posse, and we'd be on the road to meet them. I had Roy and Jake with me. They spoke the language.

Behind us everything was quiet. The sentry evidently was still tranquil, and the Sonof was still giving us time to think things over. It was that, or he was leaving us for later because he was busy with Mom. I should never have had that thought.

It made me hurry, and it made me careless. We'd come far enough so that it was a safe bet that the sentry had been a loner, no outer line of defense beyond him. I broke into a run. Coming out of the woods, I started scrambling down the slope to the road. A searchlight caught me full in the eyes, like clubbing me across the eyeballs. I couldn't see a thing, but I heard the bullet rip the air alongside my left ear. I wasn't waiting for any zeroing in. It was no good dropping, not where I was with the ground falling away in front of me. I'd land head down and spread over the slope, a target just asking to be holed. Also how do you work a tommygun when you're flat to ground that's so tilted that it has your butt a foot or more higher than your head and shoulders? You don't.

I sliced off on a zigzag course, trying to outguess the spotlight. I zigged out of the beam, but it was swinging over toward me. I whipped up the tommygun and let go. It got the light. That helped, but I still had to come down that slope to the road, and I wasn't on silent turf any more. With every step I was sending some loose rock rattling along ahead of me. Another shot came at me, and it sounded much too close. Aiming by ear isn't quite as good as getting a cat in your sights, but you never can tell when somebody's going to get lucky with it, and do well enough. I kicked my left foot out, as I zigged off at an angle to the right. The pebbles I kicked loose bounced, rattling down to the road.

Another shot went spitting into their noise. After the light in my eyes, I was still not seeing anything beyond a flock of bright green clouds, but I had to take the chance. I jumped blind. If I landed any place short of the road, I'd get me a couple of broken legs.

I made the road, but I brought a landslide with me. A shot blasted into the sound. It spun me and took me down. I was all right now. I was on the flat of the road. I was away from the loose stones, and I could move along without making all that racket. There was no light that could be put on me. I crawled toward where I'd seen the muzzle flash. I felt the warm wet on my left arm up where the muscles come down off the shoulder, but I was happy to settle for that. It was only blood. I was using the arm for crawling, and it was doing everything you ever ask an arm to do. I could move all my fingers, and the blood wasn't gushing, just oozing along my skin. It was okay. I had more where that came from.

The only thing bugging me was the sudden quiet. I couldn't hear a thing. I was considering making some noise of my own, just so I could draw a shot. I could use another muzzle flash to aim at. How far had I spun with that bullet? Could I be sure I was crawling in the right direction?

Then there was a sound. It was a thud followed by a little moan. Almost immediately a car's roadlights came on, and full in the beam of them I saw Jake running in, holding his whip handle at the ready. Roy was standing beside the car. He spoke.

"It's a dame," he gasped. "I clubbed her down—a dame."

I was scrambling to my feet.

"The battleax," Jake said. Then with quick contrition he corrected it. "Mrs. Grymm," he said. "Big deal. We got Mrs. Grymm."

"Heave her into the car," I barked, "and let's get away from here. They had to hear the shots back at the house."

I stood over her, holding the tommygun on her, while the boys were picking her up off the road. I snagged a .45 out of her hand. The revolver was still hot.

"Oughtn't we be doing something to bring her around?" Roy babbled.

"Just so somebody'll have to cool her again?" I snarled.

They wasted time being gentle about the way they lifted her into the back seat. I got in there with her. Right off I knew where I was. It isn't every Cadillac that's fitted with a bookshelf. I didn't even have to read the titles. I knew what the Sonof's French-educated brother read.

Jake slid in behind the wheel. Roy took the other seat up front.

"Hospital?" Jake asked.

"Fuzz," I said. "She'll live."

She was already beginning to stir. I don't want this to reflect unfairly on Roy's efficiency. Grymm had a lot of hair, and just where he'd clubbed her happened to be where she had the most of it. I knew where by the hole he'd put in her hairnet.

At close quarters the tommygun was too long for convenience. I held her .45 on her, having checked to make sure she hadn't spent the full load. There were still a couple of slugs in it, and I was ready to put them into her, but not until I'd made her lead me to Mom.

Alongside the bookshelf there was another compartment I knew about. It was for the Coke bottles. The brother never had anything but Coke bottles in his car because he was a good Moslem, but this brother had been to school in France. His Coke bottles were always filled with Armagnac.

Holding the revolver on her with my right hand, I used my left to bring out a bottle and pry off the cap. The arm was beginning to feel a little stiff, but not enough to put it out of commission. I was bleeding on to the brother's beautiful seat covers. I felt I couldn't give the blood in a better cause.

Her mouth was working. Ramming the neck of the bottle between her teeth, I poured. She came up sputtering. She also came up fighting. I nudged her with the muzzle of the .45, and she settled down.

"Okay, stupid," she said. "You win. Now what?"

"Where's Mom?"

"Not back at the hotel? I don't know."

"She was kidnaped. Early this morning she was kidnaped right off that crazy island."

"Talk to your man, stupid. We had nothing to do with that."

"Could be," I groaned.

It was no more than I had been thinking—that the Sonof, figuring as he was that I'd thrown in with Grymm and the brothers, took Mom for the leverage it would give him on me. I was trying to figure what Grymm and/or the brothers could have wanted with her, and I couldn't come up with anything.

"Where are we going now?" she asked.

"The fuzz."

"We can make a deal. What's to stop you? Loyalty to your man, even after he's kidnaped your mother?"

"Unless you have Mom, you have nothing to dicker with."

"You swing to me, and I can still bring this thing off. I'm getting a quarter of a million. You can split a good piece of it."

"They selling you pot?"

"I'm selling them guns. Your man's through. His brothers are taking over. I've been all day loading the guns on the ship for them. She's waiting out at sea. As soon as I collect, she sails. You can help me collect. All you do is get your man away from the house."

"How do I do that?"

"Make a deal with him. He's got your mother. Trade him. He hands her over to you, and you tell him where the guns are."

"Where do I tell him?"

"The island. Tell him they're over on the island. Get him to go over there with you."

"Up to now you've been a lot smarter than that. As soon as you heard from Mom that she had a son and where he was working and for whom, you began sucking up to her. You couldn't believe it was just a coincidence your meeting up with her like that. You began thinking maybe she was keeping an eye on you, so you played it smart. You latched on to her so you could keep an eye on her. Then you heard I was coming over to Athens, and you were sure you'd been making the right move."

"Now, look. It's a big deal. I have a lot at stake."

"Sure. So much that when Hamid came climbing down the balconies to spy on me, you thought he was after you, and the deal was big enough to make it worth pushing him off. I made the rest of it that night easy for you, leaving a drink around till I had time to drink it. You doped that drink, so you could prowl my room and search it for something that maybe would clear up where I stood. You're also a good housekeeper. You washed out the empty glass so it would show no trace of dope."

"I could have fixed that drink so I'd have had you out of my hair for good. I didn't want to hurt you."

"Thanks a million. Then there was the flashlight at the restaurant to signal your boys that I was coming out. I was going places. You wanted to know where."

"So they followed you? Did they do you any harm?"

"Then last night. My drink drugged again and my watch reset so I'd come out of it without knowing I'd been drugged, not till I got downstairs and saw a clock. You wanted even that little slice of extra time. You play it safe every which way. Snagging the trigger spring out of my pistol wasn't enough."

"No," she snarled, "it wasn't enough. I didn't like it when you picked up your tramp friends in Corinth. I had a feeling about them. They followed me up from the beach this morning, and they brought your man with them. I was hardly in the villa before he came through the front gate. I went out the back and saw to the loading."

"And now you were on the back road, waiting for one of the brothers to slip out and pay you off. We came instead."

"I should have killed you while I had the chance."

I was watching her. I wasn't watching the road. Roy brought the Cadillac to a screaming stop. More than ever I had to keep watching her.

"What's that for?" I barked. "Get going."

"Fuzz," Roy said.

Even while he was saying it, I was in Athens and the crazy thing starting all over again. Grymm's door came open. Heracles climbed in, pushed Grymm up against me, and made room for himself on the seat.

He was still settling himself when I moved. Out of the corner of my eye I could see the police cars where they were blocking the road. They weren't close enough. Either Heracles or Grymm could still get me, even under their fuzzy noses. I brought it down to even money. Using the butt end of her .45 for it, I slugged Grymm. I picked a better spot than Roy had found, one where her hair wasn't piled so thickly. She slumped against Heracles, which was fine because that tied him up long enough for me to flip the .45 around in my hand and get the muzzle leveled at him.

"Mr. Erridge," Heracles said. "I owe you a thousand apologies. They'll sound more sincere if I can make them not at gun point. I would like them to sound sincere, Mr. Erridge."

"To hell with your apologies. You kidnaped her. Where is she?"

"Your lady mother? She is safe and well. She will tell you herself she came to no harm. I took her into protective custody. I had my duty to do, Mr. Erridge, but I was able also to see to her safety."

"Who the hell are you?"

He introduced himself. Nicholas Zambelios. He added his official title, but I didn't need it. I saw the way the fuzz in the blockading cars jumped when he barked a couple of words at them. They took Grymm out of the Cadillac and hauled her to one of their cars. They fell in around us and escorted us on along the road. The big boy was fuzz, upper echelon fuzz.

He explained, and he apologized. He had rescued Mom from her traffic tangle, and he was making no secret of it. Mom turned the big lug on. When he came around to the Axilles to keep his date with her, the desk told him she had checked out and left no Athens address. She had left a note, and the Axilles didn't refuse a police officer of his eminence a glimpse of the note.

While he's considering whether to pursue the lady or not, a man comes in, and in the company of that most questionable of Spartans, Constantine Leonidas. The man claims to be the lady's son. Heracles tags him for an imposter. Can he allow this unsavory pair to know where they can find a fine lady like Mrs. Erridge? Anybody who's paired up with Kostya Leonidas is unsavory. That's axiomatic.

But, more than that, Heracles must find out what this unsavory cat is up to. Easy. He joins the man in his cab. He slugs him. He goes through his pockets. Much to Heracles's embarrassment, the cat's passport establishes that he is the lovely lady's son. Can he keep mother and son apart, even if, judging by the company he keeps, son isn't all he ought to be? He takes off, telling the cabbie to deliver son to the Queen's Palace Hotel where he will find his mama.

Unhappily for Heracles, after making a booboo of such proportions, he must avoid the lovely lady from here on out. How can he ever explain to her why he would cool her only boy with his string of worry beads? But then he's called back on duty to go around to the QP. An Egyptian visitor has plunged to his death from one of the balconies. It is routine to check the hotel register, and Heracles discovers that Leonidas had checked in shortly before the tragedy.

The fuzz go to Kostya's room. He's no longer there. They turn the room upside down, searching it, and they find there a note from Matthew Erridge. Full of sadistic promises, it says: *"Don't come to my room. I'll come to yours."* They also find in the room a reek of Lily of Luxor. The unfortunate visitor from Egypt has been in that room.

Sorry as he is to think ill of the lovely lady's son, duty tells Heracles that Erridge will bear watching. Then Erridge calls the American Embassy and talks about murder. He wants the fuzz, but when the fuzz arrives, he's passed out drunk. Nobody knows what to think of Erridge.

The next day, however, the cat is back in there wanting the fuzz again. The men he talks to have Hamid's murder in hand, but they have other problems as well. They're busy covering for Heracles. There's no way they can explain what's been going on without embarrassing him, so they cover it up instead. They bring in a phony cabbie with a phony story, and that leaves things where nobody can pin them down.

"We picked Leonidas up for the Hamid murder," Heracles told me, "but we had to release him to your employer. He said Leonidas and Hamid were both in his hire, both watching you for him. His brothers were in Greece shopping guns, and he was looking for proof that you were their agent. He accused you of murdering Hamid. We were convinced he was mistaken about you, Mr. Erridge. Yesterday, Mr. Erridge, you made a very good impression on my colleagues in Athens."

He'd gotten that far when we pulled up at the fuzz pad. He oversaw the unloading of Grymm, and then he told Roy to drive on down to the boat landing. There was a launch tied up there, and it was everything the hotel clerk said it was. Heracles escorted us down into it.

"Where are we going?" I asked, hanging back.

"To your mama, Mr. Erridge. Where else would you want to go?"

"Where is she?"

"On the yacht."

"Your yacht?"

"Your employer's yacht. I borrowed it from him for the day."

"To protect Mom? He knew that?"

"Naturally not. I wanted to protect her, not to involve her."

On board the launch he dug up a first-aid kit and insisted on dressing the scratch on my arm. It was only a short run away from the landing. We went out past the executioners' pad and closed in on a floating Versailles. It was no more than was to be expected. The Sonof always does himself well. A light from the yacht picked us up as we pulled alongside; and I was blinded again. This time what came at me wasn't gunfire. It was Mom's voice.

"Matthew," she was shouting. "Are you all right, Matthew?"

"I'm great. Are you all right?"

"Except for worry over you. What have you been up to, Matthew?"

"Not me, Mom. You. You keep bad company, kid."

"I know, but I couldn't help it. He kidnaped me."

By this time I was on my way up the companionway, and she was waiting for me at the head of it. She looked great, but right off she spotted the dressing on my arm and the blood on my shirt. She turned away from me to fix on Heracles. She wanted to know what he'd done to me.

"Not him," I told her. "Your buddy, Grymm. She deals out mickeys. She's a gun runner and a killer. Nick's got her in the pokey."

Mom wasn't letting him off. "And all day you let me worry," she said. "You could have told me it wasn't Matthew you were after."

He made to soothe her down with one of those pats. It was the wrong move. She pivoted away from it, and it was a double-duty pivot. It put her full body weight behind the smack she fetched him square across the chops. It was a good smack, but it didn't even rock Heracles.

"Not half of what I deserve," he said. "I'm still apologizing. Yesterday evening we were convinced your boy was not involved in any of these troubles." He turned back to me. "We were working with your boss, and we located his brothers for him. They were here. He came down, but the next we hear is that you're heading this way, too. Why here of all places?"

The way he's got to read it, the Sonof is right about me, after all. That doesn't bug him too much. It makes me merely illegal, and he's going to have to do his duty, but that's all in the day's work. What does mildew his yoghurt is me bringing Mom along. Why that, unless I'm using her and Grymm as a screen? That's worse than illegal. I'm the kind of fink he's going to love bringing in, but first he's got to kidnap Mom, just for her own good.

"What about Mrs. Grymm?" I asked. "You didn't want to protect her?"

Heracles took offense at the question. "Look at your mama," he said, "and remember what Mrs. Grymm looks like. You won't ask such questions."

So Mom was taken into protective custody, and the island was watched. All I had to do was show, and they were set to tail me; but the whole morning wore away and I gave them nothing. When I did appear, mounted on the ramparts of the executioners' pad, they thought to catch me signaling, but nothing.

There was only one thing they could figure. They'd lost Roy and Jake. I had to be playing it smart, sitting tight on the ramparts of the pad, keeping all the fuzz surveillance fixed on me while the kids carried the ball.

"With all this surveillance?" I asked. "How come you didn't know Grymm came ashore?"

"We knew," he said ruefully, "but who pays attention? The old ladies with the white gloves and the hairnets, we have them all the time. They get up to climb the hills and see the sun rise. They're out in the fields to collect wildflowers. All through the night you find them all over the country. They sit on ruins and try to read Lord Byron by moonlight."

About the time I came ashore, a police cutter out at sea picked up the ship Grymm had been loading. The fuzz boarded her and took over, and the search for Roy and Jake went into higher gear. If not the kids, they could think of only one other possibility. Mom's fuzzy admirer, old Nick, headed up to the villa to check with the Sonof. Did the Sonof have all the brothers under his thumb? Had even one of them been loose any time during the day? Was he certain it was only this sextet and that none of the others out of his legion of brothers was involved?

Nick was on his way up out of the town when he heard the shooting on the back road. He came to investigate that while some of his men went on to the villa just in time to find the Sonof stampeding down to the cellar to check on us. Just as he was meeting up with us on the road, Nick on his car radio had the word from the villa. None of the brothers had been out of the house all day, and in the moment of stress the Sonof let slip the one thing the fuzz hadn't known. He'd had Roy and Jake with him all day as well.

"So nobody was on the loose to see to the loading of that gun runner," Nick said. "Even then I didn't think of the old lady. I had her sitting on a ruin some place reading her poetry, and I never thought she would read the parts of Lord Byron ladies never hear about."

"But when you came on us," I said, "you were completely hep."

He chuckled. "She was different then," he said. "She didn't have the little white gloves on."

More seriously he explained that, once he recognized Grymm for what she was, all that had been impossible suddenly became possible. It came clear for him just as it had for me. The drinks that couldn't possibly have been doped now could all too easily have been doped. Everything clicked.

The Sonof and his brothers were firmly invited out of the country. They left; and the Sonof, again behaving traditionally, scattered largesse in his wake. He sent me a Cadillac and went off to find himself another engineer. Roy and Jake got checks that were fatter than they could believe. They also got to keep the whips, but protocol said they couldn't use them where they would have done the most good. Nick Zambelios finally got it made. He took Mom out to show her the Athens tourists never see.

When I said goodby to Roy and Jake, I asked them where they were heading now they had all that bread of the Sonof's.

"Mount Athos," they said. They read my face. "Just on our way out of the country," they explained. "We keep thinking of the ratfinks we came in with and how they've been freeloading on those monks ever since. That was when we started the thumbing, when we dug the way that deal went. We want to drop off a contribution at the monasteries, and if our old buddies are still here, maybe we could show them how our souvenirs work."

So now, Charlie, does anybody need a Cadillac equipped with

a refrigerator full of Coke? Mom doesn't want it, and Erridge goes steady with his Porsche.

About Mom's date with her Herculean fuzz, I asked her how many times in the course of the evening he patted her.

"Matthew," she said, "he's really very nice. Nicholas is a perfect gentleman, Matthew."

Maybe I'll go around to that gunshop for another fitting. Maybe I can be a perfect gentleman, since Mom says I'm very nice, too.